My Gypsy Soul, by Kelli Lee Mistry

Prologue

I am going to tell you a story, it is my story, yet, it is not. I have lived many lifetimes and this story is from my life as a Gypsy girl. I spent a year doing regression therapy while under hypnosis, trying to find the root cause of emotional distress in this lifetime; during one of the sessions I was introduced to my life as Crystobella Franco. I lived with my father, Claude Franco and we were itinerants, or peripatetic travellers. Some called us gypsies, tramps, witches, thieves, quacks, or snake oil salesmen; although we did not sell snake oil, it was actually a great natural curative, but unfortunately hard to get as it is an Asian cure-all. We grew most of our herbal tinctures here in France, and they had curative properties based on the homeopathic rule of like cures like.

I am getting ahead of myself though. I would not have known about Crystobella, had Claude not become attached to me through that lifetime and subsequently many of my past lifetimes, as well as this one. I was living in Mexico at the time in a small rented house when I became aware to the presence of Claude. One hot afternoon I had fallen asleep on my bed only to awaken and find I was in a sleep paralysis, my heart racing, with a shadowy figure standing over me. Now, fully awake, yet, unable to move, I gazed at the figure who resembled smoke, but was clearly shaped as a human man. He saw my open eyes and state of shock, then slowly turned and floated out of the doorway to the bedroom. I was shaken. I had thoughts of calling

someone, but who? Ghost Busters? It was an absurd thought, but it kept going through my mind. I finally realized I had regained use of my body and got up to check the house. I found nothing disturbed in any room: although the dog was cowering in the living room beside the couch.

I was still weak from the incident and decided to take my dog with me into the bedroom; she refused to go in, literally bracing her paws on the door jamb and refusing to enter. She maintained her position of refusing to enter that room for the next six months. Then, one day a woman came to visit me with a mutual friend, and she said she was a white witch. She used the restroom which was located on the other side of my bedroom which she had to pass through. She asked me if there had been a spirit here, in my room. I explained the situation to her and she said to light a white candle and ask for a blessing over the room. After doing this my dog walked right in and lay down by my bed, never refusing to enter the room again.

I have never forgotten the incident, but it was not foremost in my mind after some time had passed. I moved from the house that it had occurred in and I was living in a home I had purchased; I was in the process of re-doing this place. I often had odd happenings in the house, especially with guests. I called a friend who was a professed medium and asked her to please help as my ghost problems were scaring my guests and terrifying my Chihuahua. At night the spirit would hurl the crystals which I hung in the windows to deter spirits, at us! Obviously, they were ineffective, at least with this ghost. Often the Chihuahua would have a look of horror on his face and he would run and hide, with no apparent reason for him to do so.

Chapter One

One night my niece and her boyfriend were sleeping in the guest room and at about four in the morning knocked on my bedroom door. I asked what was wrong and her boyfriend said that he had had a dream about an ugly old woman with a unibrow; she popped into his face and it woke him and then his camera clicked and the flash went off as it fell from the shelf it was sitting on. He was visibly shaken as was my niece. That was the last straw; unibrow had to go!

My friend Cheryl who works as a medium came over and assessed the situation. As she was telling me about the woman who was an unwanted guest in my home, she turned away from me and said to someone I could not see, "You will have to wait until I am done with her. It will soon be your turn."

I asked incredulously, "Who are you speaking to?"

And she said, "A man named Claude. He says he is your father and wants to tell you something."

"Oh boy, more than one ghost?" I felt like I should have a little machine where the ghosts could take a number like you do at the DMV. I guess I should not have been surprised by this as my house was built near a mangrove that once had been a sacred site of the Maya. There was most likely a revolving door to the spirit world somewhere within it. Or a portal to the underworld perhaps?

Cheryl explained that the first spirit was a woman who used to live in the house and care for the owner, an older gentleman that was gravely ill. He passed on and shortly after so did she. She did not like anyone being in her house and wanted us to leave, especially the perros susios (dirty dogs) as she called them. I asked Cheryl, "Can you please let her know that this is now my house and she is the one that needs to go." I could not believe I was bargaining with a ghost about living in my own house.

Cheryl said, "The woman will not leave nor will she enter the light." She suggested I give her a job. We came to an agreement that unibrow could watch over the house as she always had, but under one condition, well actually two; she must not bother the dogs or guests and she had to stay in the carport. She agreed that this was acceptable as she could see all of the comings and goings from there. Shortly after this agreement I had an intruder and wondered why she had not done her job . . . maybe because he entered through the back door? Luckily, he only wanted to take a shower, riffle through my underwear, and watch a little television by the traces left behind. He had even re-hung his wet towels. Chimi, the chihuahua, was home ad must have entertained him! No harm was done.

Back to our ghost negotiations, it was now Claude's time to talk. He told Cheryl that he was my father and he had done something terrible to me and because of his past actions he vowed to stay with me and watch over me. Our exchange went something like this:

Claude (speaking through Cheryl): "When you were young, I made you read fortunes for people while working in the circus, even though you did not want to do it, I exploited your gifts."

Me: "This makes sense as to why I now have a block in my psychic abilities. I am actually relieved that you did not abuse me sexually though, as that was what first came to mind."

Claude: "Never would I have done such a thing! I will stay and protect you in every lifetime."

Me: "No, please go into the light, it will make me happy if you do so."

Claude: "I must protect you."

Me: "No, you must enter the light, please. I forgive you and I love you. This would make me happy."

Claude: "Okay."

Cheryl explains, "He just hugged you."

"Oddly I had felt him. It felt as if a chill passed through me."

She said, "Yes, he then left."

I felt relieved that he entered the light, or so I thought.

Chapter Two

Fast forward to about six years and I now have moved back to the states and I am living in Michigan. I still am working on healing from a divorce earlier in my life and decide that regression therapy may be the way to go. I began my search for a person that could do the hypnosis. I found Amelia Bartow. She was round and dark and reminded me of a gypsy. Better yet, she was a psychologist. We set up appointments for three sessions. She demanded cash in advance and for this, she gave a discount of thirty dollars. I thought that was nice of her, but did I really have a choice?

On the first session I went under easily, I was still aware of my surroundings and her voice guiding me through many stages of many lifetimes. There were various lives shown to me and in all of them, I was a strong woman. In most, I was alone and had to take care of myself and/or my children without a man in my life. In one life, I was a prostitute after the death of my husband as I had two lovely little girls I had to care for. We lived in the English countryside in a cottage and had been farmers before my husband's death. I found myself selling my body on the streets of London after he passed and I was amazed at the size of my breasts! This life was otherwise unremarkable and we fast forwarded to my death: I was in my room at the cottage and my daughters were there holding my hand as I passed from that lifetime. I saw myself go back to source and it was so beautiful that I could not believe that we actually came back to the earth for other lifetimes, but we must, as here I was, again living on the earth in my earth suit, (my word for skin).

Amelia guided me through several more lifetimes, and they did not really have anything to show me that would allow me to heal in this lifetime. I felt that I needed to look at this lifetime, maybe my childhood, but try as we might, I would not go there; I would travel to any other place or lifetime but this one. On one occasion I was in this gorgeous garden and it turned out to be the center of the Earth, I was visiting Mother Earth! She was so beautiful and surrounded by a garden full of flowers, plants, and creatures, and in the center was a huge, light green crystal tower! I was mesmerized and wished I could live here, but Amelia led me back up the stone stairs and through the ornate iron gate leading out of the garden, and there I sat; in the comfortable, drab chair, in this lifetime once again: with no further knowledge on how to help myself become whole again.

The next visit I told her would be my last and I requested looking into my life with Claude Franco. Amelia got me to go under and led me to that lifetime . . . It was in France, just outside of Paris, it looked like an era between the fifteen-hundreds and the eighteen-hundreds. I could not be sure as I was a young woman, dressed as a gypsy. I was maybe fourteen or fifteen years of age, I had long dark wavy hair, it shone with purple and blue streaks in the sun like the wing of a raven. My features were interesting, I had a strong nose and high cheekbones, the bone structure of my face was exquisite, almost royal but not quite, my chin was not strong or weak and the curve of my jaw lent to the oval shape of my face, my top lip was slightly larger than the bottom lip, but they were full and a beautiful plum color, my brows were thick and as dark as my hair, yet, my eyes were a blue-green, almost grey, and shone like jewels.

My dress was a white and grey cotton petticoat with butterfly wing sleeves and ruffles on the edges. I was wearing an intricately made white lace apron as was the custom of the times when Marie Antoinette ruled the country. I had a beautiful scarf wrapped around my waist and over my shoulder; it looked like it came from Spain or another foreign place. There was only a small locket around my neck, no earrings that you would normally see on gypsy women, but I did have many rings on my fingers and they all had some type of gemstone in them; I recognized one as moonstone.

I looked at my surroundings: I saw that I was sitting by a small fire near a wagon; it was the typical barrel shape of the itinerants, the travellers. Back then it was termed a bow-top. There were two horses tied by the wagon and chickens running about. I was cooking something. I marveled at the wagon and all of the unique items hanging upon it: there were many herbs tied in bundles hanging from the side, drying in the sun. The ribbons from which they were strung were pretty and varied in color adding to the patchwork look of the camp.

I reached for a pot hanging near the door and knocked over a handmade straw broom, after picking it up, I turned back to the fire and began to cook eggs in a bit of butter. I grabbed a thick cloth and removed the kettle that had begun to boil, adding some water to my herbal mixture in a chipped china teapot on the table beside the wagon. The table was covered in different scarves with tassels and fringe hanging down and the wooden chairs next to it were old and weathered, tattered pillows flung upon the seats. A light breeze rustled the herbs on the side of the wagon, sending a beautiful fragrance into the air. I loved this life, I was so happy, yet . . . I did not smile, in fact I looked forlorn as I cooked. As soon as this thought crossed my mind, I felt as if Crystobella and I became one . . . I was no longer experiencing a past life I was living it.

In the distance, I could hear my father calling for me. "Crystobella!"

"I am here Papa," I yelled back, hearing an echo ring across the field. He came up and embraced me in a huge hug. He called them his papa bear hugs, and I was his baby bear. I hated being called that, but tolerated it as it seemed to make him happy.

"Crystobella, we must travel tonight as there is big faire going on near Versailles in two days' time."

"But Papa, I am happy here, please may we stay here for a while? We have the Cirque every weekend and the market midweek. I have just gathered many herbs to make my remedies. People count on me to be at the mark ---"

Papa rudely cut me off. "Baby Bear, you know that we are travellers, our bread and butter come from fresh blood, new clients. You have a wonderful gift and sharing it with the world is necessary! Think of all the people you help with your insight."

He pulled something from his satchel and it shone in the sunlight. It was the most beautiful crystal ball I had ever laid eyes upon!

"This is for you Baby Bear; you must look the part of a fortune teller if you are to impress the people in Versailles! We will charge a bit more to cover the cost of this and your new scarf with the galbi fringe."

"Papa, I do not care to use my gifts to read fortunes for people, a gift from the creator should be used to heal and shared without cost just as we are provided for, we shall provide for others."

"Dear naïve Crystobella, where do such fantasies arise from? Have you been conversing with your dearly departed puri daj again?"

"But Papa, she had much wisdom and she still shares it with me from the other side. I must listen to her and heed her warnings to use caution. Misusing a gift is the way to bad karma. There is another reason I would like to stay . . . Marcello needs me to make him a tincture for his fits. I must ---"

"Crystobella! That is enough! You shall do as your father says! Now serve me my eggs dear child."

"Yes, Papa."

Oh, how I despised my father when he would take advantage of my gifts. When mama was alive, he would never have gotten away with such atrocities. My dya was a very exotic creature with great spiritual gifts. She could "see" with her third eye. She often could tell what was to come before it actually occurred. Yet, she knew that keeping things to herself was often best unless it would help the greater good. She instilled in me her morals and sense of integrity; I often wonder how she and Papa ever became a couple! He is out for himself and no one else!

I knew I must do as he said. "I shall be ready to leave soon."

Claude Franco was a handsome beng, she'd give him that; he was rugged looking, with a broad nak, not quite regal, just like her nose, she could not deny her heritage. He also had high cheekbones and long, dark, wavy hair, the same blue-black as hers. He had deep-set eyes of the darkest brown; she gathered they matched his soul! His lashes were long and his eyebrows straight and thick. He had full lips and a slight gap in his teeth, but that just added to his charm.

Women fell at his feet. I suppose that is how my mother ended up with him. Now that her mama and grandmamma were gone, she was left to deal with him alone. My paternal puri daj protected me from Claude the best she could, but she passed on when I was a girl, just about to turn ten, so I have been alone with Papa now for about six years.

I pulled a worn sheet of paper out of the posoti in my skirt, it was a drawing of my family, done when my dya was pregnant with me, she was standing next to Claude and his mother, and she had the happy look of a young girl that has gotten her first taste of love. Her smile beamed off of the paper at me, my mama was named Clara Anne, and everyone loved her. She had exotic looks that made men do crazy things. Her eyes were large and almond shaped, her bal straight and black, it was worn in braids most of the time; She had beautifully shaped lips, with the upper lip being just a bit plumper than the lower; I was glad I had something of my mother's, we shared the same beautiful lips.

My mother wore many beads around her neck and galbi dangled from her braids; they must have made the most beautiful tinkling when she moved. Like her daughter, she did not wear the typical gypsy hoops in her ears but had many rings made from gemstones that held meaning for her according to my puri daj. She wore a band around her head with a jewel exactly where her third eye is located. It was an emerald and matched her eyes. Such beauty and gone too soon from this earthly plane. Of course, the drawing was in charcoal, but grandmamma had told me many times the color of the clothes and the vibrancy of my mother's jewels, now they were forever in my memory.

I took my eyes off of my mother and gazed at my puri daj's depiction. My grandmother was one of the most beautiful women in our band during her younger days, yet, in this photo that beauty only came from the soul shine twinkling through her eyes. She had the grey hair of an old wise one, worn like her daughter-in-law, braided. She only wore one strand of beads where her daughter-in-law wore many. She was dressed in an array of floral designs, none of which matched, her shirt belled out on the sleeves and she wore a bandana tied around her head, her face was lined from the life she had lived, like a map. The lines around her mouth being the deepest as she perpetually sucked on an ornate pipe, and in her arms, she held her old marmalade machka, Josiah. My grandmother was a character, but a strong woman that held the wisdom of the ages within her soul.

My grandmamma always spoke Romanes, the ancient language of the gypsies; saying, "We must keep our traditions alive." Often, I would be asked to translate for her with customers, even though my grandmamma knew how to speak other languages such as the Queen's English, French, and Spanish, she refused to do so. I am proud that my grandmother gave to me the gift of my heritage.

Many thought that Gypsies came from Egypt, hence the name Gypsies, or Gyps. Yet, we actually are originally from India and Syria. We are a misunderstood race and have endured many hardships, persecution and death because of the heritage we are so proud of. We are the nomads, the tinkers, and the craftsman. Why was it such a crime to be a Gypsy? *I would not want to be anything else, even if I could be*, I thought. I am so proud to be of the Romnipen.

I pulled another drawing from my posoti, my grandmamma was tarneder in this one and my father was a small boy, he had those same dark eyes, and there was a leather band worn around his forehead. He had on a hand knitted sweater; it had bands of different colors as if it had been knitted from leftover yarn scraps. He had the same broad nose and high cheekbones, although they were covered in a layer of baby fat . . . he looked mischievous. Beside him at a table sat his mother in all of her glory! She was breathtaking, with a beauty that went deeper than her skin; it was as deep as her soul.

Her eyes were large and deep, they were a beautiful amber color, or so I had been told, the photos were charcoal and faded. My grandmother was called Rosa lee, she had the most perfect bow shaped lips, and they were glossy in the photo. Her eyes lined with kohl gave her a mysterious look. Her nak was regal and her cheekbones high. Her eyebrows were thick and framed her eyes well. She wore a jeweled headband that dipped into a vee just between her eyes, with one large jewel hanging down over her third eye. I imagined it must have been a ruby, for that would have suited such a fine woman.

There was a silk veil draped over her head yet it only enhanced my grandmother's lush head of wavy brown bal flowing to her mashakar. Large pearl earrings dangled from her lobes, her hands were crossed in front of her, just under her chin, her elbows resting on the table, and her gaze was intense, magical! I could see myself in this face and I felt blessed that my puri daj continued to advise me from beyond the grave. Also, feeling blessed that my nano, Vano was such a gifted artist, it was rare for gypsies to have portraits of their loved ones such as these.

My puri daj had held on to them for many years, tucked safely away under a hidden panel in her jewelry box. Shortly before her passing she took them out and gave them to me; telling me during every visit there after all of the details in the drawings, the colors, the moods, and especially the virtues that each person held. I cherish these memories and know they would not last if I did not find a place to keep them safe. I shall ask Marcello to make a wooden box with a hidden panel; he is an accomplished woodworker, using his creative imagination to design fine pieces that are sold to aristocrats and royalty, as well as to the commoners at the markets. He has quite a reputation as an artisan.

Claude's yell tore me from my daydreams.

"Yes, Papa, I have your dinner ready." I put the eggs on the plate, slightly overdone, but he never seemed to complain about my cooking. I often daydreamed and overcooked our food, maybe he was used to it. At least the eggs were fresh, gathered that morning from the khania. I added herbed potatoes with sir to the plate and a chunk of bread I had traded for at the market last week. I kept it fresh by compressing it. It was a trick used by travellers so that bread could last up to a month or more. The bread was fermented and then it was stacked in cast iron pans in an oven that was heated at around two hundred degrees Fahrenheit where it was slowly dried to remove excess moisture: this was done so that it would not crack, then it was left to cool and carefully compressed. Compressing the bread with pressing plates makes it easier to carry and store. If you preferred plump bread you could add a bit of water to it and it would swell considerably. Papa always ate it compressed and he loved the herb bread the best.

I had lost my appetite and decided to go and get the horses bedded down for the night as they would have to be hitched up in a few hours' time, taking them on a journey to the new faire grounds. It would take us at least a day if all went smoothly, but most likely with the vardo and only the two horses to pull it, will take longer and we have to arrive at Versailles before two days pass. It is almost forty-five kilometers from where we are right now, just outside of Paris. I better pack up the wares and secure the herbs adre, it would take some time to hang them from the ceiling beams. "Aaah . . ." I sighed; *I feel like a servant most of the time!*

Later I sat in one of the chairs and smoked a hand-rolled herbal cigarette. I was thinking that smoking is such a nasty habit, but it is what all the gypsies do. One thing about the Romani people you can bet on is that they love their tobacco and their alcohol.

The chere were brilliant tonight and the shon was just a crescent, as the new moon had just passed a couple of days back. I know that the shon affects people's emotions, but I give more power to the Kham, for me the sun is the creation energy and the sustaining force for all living beings. It gives you vitamin D and maintains the balance of the mind so that a person does not get depressed. I was not sure how it worked, exactly, but I know that the animals react to the light and the dark and that some hormones are affected by sunlight and darkness. During solar eclipses often animals would lie down and rest thinking it was night time. I always made time to sit in the sun and loved the bronze look it gave my skin. Winters often were harsh and I would begin to feel sad, but luckily spring would return once more and the balance was restored.

Chapter Three

I knew I was a knowledgeable herbalist and often I heard people whisper at the market that I must be a witch as they say my herbal tinctures worked magick. I did not like people thinking I am a chovexani. After all, I never sold draba or cast spells; I am a healer just like my grandmamma before me. I help people. I also know the penalties a person faced if one were accused of witchcraft, sometimes it was a flogging or a branding, depending on the decree of the king who was ruling at the time, or it could be death by drowning or beheading, or the worst fate, burning at the stake. I had heard a tale about twenty-six Gypsies being beheaded in Giessen, Hesse. Some were beheaded and the rest were hanged. Their crime was that they were born a Gypsy and unfortunately lived in Germany where being Gypsies was a crime. Of course, these rules and laws were enacted because the guilds did not like their earnings being undercut by nomadic men and if the Roma did not have addresses, they would not have to pay taxes. It made me sad to think that there was so much bloodshed . . . in the name of greed.

I was told many times that I was a heathen, a godless and wicked prostitute. This confused me as I am very spiritual and love God; my belief is Ma-sha-llah, as God wills. Of course, there were bands of Gypsies that were considered mizhak, they were horse thieves and the children were taught to pick pockets while their mothers, grandmothers, or aunts read fortunes! This was not my heritage, my people, I came from a line of trustworthy healers, well, all except . . . maybe my father. I had to give him credit though as he had love for his daughter's gifts, and they were real gifts. He may charge a price but I told them the truth; it is only fair to speak chachimos. The people were getting a fortune of truth which came from above, at least.

Gypsy culture has many traditions, most coming from the old country; one I especially despised was that of the "arranged marriage", my father was always on the lookout for a good dom for me, although he knew I would have to live with the husband's familia and do household chores for them, so he never tried too hard to actually make this happen lest he be left to fend for himself.

I also knew that when a person passed to the spirit realm, they were considered a mulo and all of their belongings were to be destroyed so that the dead did not haunt the living. I would be in trouble if my Papa found out I had my grandmother's drawings. That was why I needed to meet Marcello soon. It would have to wait now until our return from Versailles. I loved Marcello but kept that hidden from my father too, as Marcello is much older than my fifteen and a half years on this earth. He was twenty-eight and my father would kill us both if he knew of our love.

Well, the camp was packed up and the groi cared for so they would be ready to travel in the wee hours of the morning. Papa said, "tonight", but he never made it home before dawn. I best get to bed now so I will be up in time to get us moving. My father always drank late into the night making music with his buddies, gambling, or was in the company of women. It would be up to me to get the horses moving while he slept it off in his bunk. *Maybe an arranged marriage would not be so bad after all* I thought! My second thought was; *well, it could be jumping from the pan into the yog, as one never knows what the future holds.*

I had a fitful sov with vivid dreams during the night. I dreamt I was married to an old man and I was wearing tattered clothing as I slaved over the fire cooking and doing the laundry. My father was nearby with a chest of gold and he was letting it fall from his fingers as he looked upon me and laughed. I should get my mind right before bed from now on; going to bed with anger was not good for my beauty rest. I also prayed last night's dream was not prophetic, as my dreams often were.

Chapter Four

Time to get the horses hitched and be on our way. I checked on my father and as I suspected he smelled of rum and was still snoring. It will be up to me to get us there on time, once again!

The horses were a Friesian mix of dark brown colour and they had some white on their leg feathering. I brushed them as they ate and then gently donned the harnesses. I had named my beloved beasts Ganache and Madeleine, basically after French pastries, but they were fitting names as Ganache was a dark chocolate color and Madeleine, although she is the same dark brown as her partner, she is a golden girl, a golden cake. We bred the pair this year and I decided the resulting foal will be called Mousse. Oh, how I love my horses! I only wish I could find a way to bottle their scent, it was heavenly to my senses.

Once the team was hitched, I hopped up onto the bench and hollered giddy-up. The pair trudged along up the hill towards the main roadway. It shall be a long ride, and I hope my father will be able to relieve me at some point in our travels. Versailles was only about fifteen kilometers from Paris proper, to the Southwest, yet, the Gypsy camp was about forty kilometers to the Northeast of Paris and Versailles was in the opposite direction. I knew the route would be long and boring as we had to travel the outskirts of the grand city of Paris.

The team plodded along as the French countryside passed us by. I saw a series of ramshackle farms that had popped up recently. The small agricultural farms are owned by peasants and are termed half-profits, they are stepping-stones for hired laborers to become capitalists, or "la culture a mi-fruits", which is simply hectares with peasant owners. To me, they look like plots of misery for which the landowners are ever indebted to the Royals. The people looked miserable and unhappy as well. I know that I prefer the nomadic life to that. I never want to be a slave to a piece of land just to make the wealthy fatter.

The closer we came toward Versailles the more the landscape was favorable to my gaze. I saw new cottages and villas with beautiful flowers over their arched gates. I passed a vast onion field, and then came upon a small town with grapes clustered on the city walls, and a quaint little roadside stand selling fruits and vegetables. I decided to stop for some fruit and thrust my hand into my dress posoti for a few coins. I chose a perfectly ripe peach; as I bit into it a drop of juice ran down my chin and the vendor reached out to wipe it away for me. He was an intense looking fellow with a mean grin. I instinctively jerked back.

He said, "What is wrong with you putain gitane?!"

I did not like this word that translated to Gypsy whore. As I turned to get back into the vurdon, the man grabbed me from behind and tried to undo my skirt. As I cried out my father appeared from adre the bow-top and leaped to the ground grabbing the man and knocking him to his knees.

I was visibly shaken and was grateful for my father's presence this time. I ran to him and hugged him, "Oh, Papa, he is a horrible man, a shilmulo!"

My father helped me onto the wagon. He sat beside me and took the lines. The man was dusting himself off as we pulled away.

I said, "Thank you," to my father and handed him a peach from the bag I still held in my hands.

"I am not hungry, Baby Bear." He continued to drive the team. He was staring straight ahead.

"I am so grateful for you helping me back there, Papa. I did not do anything; he just came at me. I was so frightened of him; he had such an evil scowl."

"Now, now, Baby Bear, it will be alright. Don't worry; I know you did nothing to provoke that man. Some men are just monsters. I am glad that I was here with you; had you been alone . . . I shall not even think about what would have happened. I think we shall avoid that town on future travels as they shall never believe us, Gypsies, over the townsfolk." He put the lines in one hand and patted my knee with his free hand. "Your Papa Bear will always protect you, my sweet angel."

My father may be many things, but he did adore me and he did always protect me. Maybe his forcing me to read fortunes is just a survival mechanism which he employs. I really do not mind it so much, I just feel cheap when I tell people their future and even though I was normally correct, no one can truly tell the future. If they say they can, they are lying. I could guess what would occur in a person's life based on their energy at the time of the reading and the information they provided, but truly telling the future, no.

The thing I dislike the most is that my suggestions for their future would almost cement that version in their mind and so it would come to pass. For me, this was bibaxt, bad luck, or negative karma. I so wish Papa would allow me to sell my herbal tinctures instead. He told me that they took too much time and did not bring the price that being a drabarno brought to us. It was for this reason, I always wore my bujo, my medicine bag protected me from evil. I often wanted to give bujos to the clients, but my father would not hear of it, but maybe if I could sell them for a price, he would allow it.

I decided to make as many bujos as possible and get them filled with the necessary herbs for protection and I could then offer these to my clients with a small crystal stone for protection. This may bring kintala in the karmic scales for my binos. My bujo was always hidden out of sight, which is the way to use medicine magick, to keep it hidden and personal. I feel that this gives it more power. Magick was taught to me by my grandmother and she cautioned to use if for good, to do no harm. The day my puri daj gave me the medicine bag she also instructed me on how to use it. She told me that it must be kept sacred, a secret, to be powerful. I felt the truth in my grandmother's wisdom and have always kept mine hidden. I reached into my pocket to feel the comfort of my bujo, only to realize it was missing. Oh no! I must have dropped it when I was at the fruit stand; either when I pulled out the coins to pay or when I jerked away from the shimulo! I must go back to get it, but how to tell Papa?

I became very withdrawn and quiet. After some time, my father asked me, "Has the machka gotten your cheeb?"

I decided to muster up the courage to tell him about the pouch. I explained, "It was from your mother and very dear to me." I begged him to return to the small town.

"My dear child if we go back there, we are only asking for trouble. We must not stray from our journey we are already going to be behind schedule for the faire." He could see her pakvora muj turn dark and sad. He did not like to let her down, he felt as if he did that often enough. "I shall stop there on our return journey and we can search for your pouch." With his words, her face transformed and shone once more. How beautiful she was and how she looked like her dya when she was baxtalo! How he missed his sweet angel of a monashay, he was a different man when in her presence; he wished Crystobella could have known him then. The man he has become is only half the man he was when he was with Clara by his side.

Chapter Five

The rest of the trip was uneventful. The lungo drom was endless it seemed and time passed slowly; it felt tortuous to me. I was grateful to my father for agreeing to go back and look for my medicine bag. Sometimes he surprised me and I could see his heart shine through, unfortunately, that was not all of the time. His moments of softness were rare. I decided to let him know my idea to make bujos for the clients to purchase. "Papa, I came up with an idea that will bring in some extra money."

"Well, out with it then!?

"I just, well, I thought that it might be nice to offer bujos to the clients, you know medicine bags. I will charge a bit more if they want them filled with drab, the herbs. I will tell them it will offer protection, but they must keep them secret, that makes the magic stronger. This is tacho, but also will keep me safe from accusations of being a chovexani. I know that it will work as I already am able to sell my lotions, soaps, tinctures, and potions safely at the tan. Yes . . . at times people say they work magick and call me a witch behind my back, but they must know my heart is zuhno."

"Crystobella, you must know that not all have the gift to see a pure heart. I shall grant your wish to make the pouches and perhaps you can make one for yourself?"

"Whatever for, Papa?"

"To bring a husband, a tumnimos, once you are betrothed you can plan your wedding!"

"Oh, Papa! I am not interested in becoming a wife! I like being a drabarni! Besides I may already have a suitor."

"Would this be anyone I know? I pray that he is not a gajo! Fore this will bring gajengi baxt upon the familia! I wish to have a zhamutro!"

"Oh, Papa, stop! You certainly cannot believe in the old darane svatura!" I thought how I and Marcello had already shared yekhipe, and how Papa would kill us both if he ever found us out.

Claude became quiet for a few moments and then he replied to his daughter. "I shall not allow you to speak ill of our ways. You are my child and I am the phuro, you shall show me respect and you shall show the Romania respect. Do you understand, Bella?"

"Yes, Papa." I felt as if he had slapped me even though Claude will never, and has never, ever done so. He is almost always gentle where I am concerned. I told him, "I am tired and will go adre to have a rest."

He nodded. "Okay, we should arrive in a few more hours and I will need your help with the ofisa and with the groy."

I nodded my head as I slipped into the wagon.

I lay on my bunk staring at the ceiling, my Papa had allowed me to paint chere on the black barrel ceiling. I liked to imagine myself floating through those stars on a great adventure. It was my paramitsha that was told to me by my grandmother. The folktale went as such:

> A young pakvora gypsy woman fell asleep under a night sky and as she slumbered her soul left on a golden thread and soared through the milky way. During her travels in the galaxy, she happened upon a rinkeni gypsy man. Their eyes met and they knew, knew their destinies were intertwined. They joined as one and became the brightest star in the milky way for all of mankind to see.

This gives hope that true love exists for the people. I wish I was there right now shining as brightly as could be with Marcello, my one true love. I slowly drifted off to sleep as I gazed upon my wo-man-made galaxy.

I was awakened by the sudden jolt of the wagon stopping as Papa yelled, "Whoa."

I emerged from my Sanctuary to see Versailles in all of its glory! We had arrived at Quartier Saint Louis, a wonderful place full of market stalls near the construction site of the baroque inspired cathedral, it was near completion, and I thought it was amazing with its domed roof and spires. The jewel of Versailles: the palace was opulent with a maze of gardens and fountains that were a wonder of engineering. They were only turned on for special occasions as the water supply was scarce, but oh, how grand they were! My favorite of course, was the one with horses charging through the water, I loved it! I also loved the tan stalls and smelled pastries nearby. "Papa, may we have pastries and kafa for breakfast?"

"Baby Bear, that is a luxury we cannot afford."

"Please Papa, may we splurge just this once, we are surrounded by such grandeur, and I feel like a queen!"

"My sweet angel, I cannot deny you." He threw her a few coins and she wandered to the patisserie.

I chose a sweet cake stuffed with bananas and strawberries for myself and a croissant de chocolat' for my father, asking the clerk to package them up. I looked at the selection of kafas and decided upon café aulait for both myself and my papa. I promised the owner of the patisserie to return the cups when we were finished and heard him murmur 'damn Gypsies' under his breath. I hurried out of the door before he could stop me.

"Aaaah, Baby Bear, you chose well but how did you bring the kafa? The shoppe owner allowed you, a gypsy to take his wares?"

"Yes, Papa, I promised I shall return them promptly when we are finished. I must have a trustworthy face."

"My little Baby Bear, you have the face of an angel." He kissed her on her forehead and began to unload the supplies so they could set up shop.

"I will return the cups to the patisserie, Papa, and be right back to help you."

"Sure, Baby Bear, go."

The owner had a look of surprise on his face when I returned. "Here are your cups, sir. Thank you for being so kind." He nodded his head and grumbled what sounded like a thank you, but I could not be sure.

I began helping my father set up as soon as I returned. I made a beautiful display with my bujos and herbs, they were hanging on ribbons, surrounding my small table, the new crystal ball was set as the center-piece, and I felt it looked every bit as opulent in my small ofisa as the palace must look.

My father looked pleased as he said, "Pakvora, Baby Bear!"

"I went into the bow-top to get ready. I applied kohl to my eyes and brushed my eyebrows, I put my new scarf on. I was ready. I looked into the mirror at the finished product, and I could not believe how beautiful and wise I looked. *Pakvora indeed,* I thought.

I checked on the horses and saw that Ganache had thrown one of his petalos. Now I would have to work extra hard to pay the ferari to reset him with a new one. Best I must get to my tent now rather than later.

"Papa, we must find a blacksmith. . ." I realized I was speaking to thin air; Papa was most likely off drinking and gambling somewhere! I entered my ofisa and began a meditation. I thought my father is the reason we have such prikasa!

My first customer arrived only moments later; a tall dark stranger, and a very handsome one at that. "Please have a seat, sir," I said while motioning to the chair at the side of the table. I was mesmerized by his eyes. They were deep pools of blue, the color of the sky. I realized I had been staring at him and stuttered, "Uh, well, umm, shall we begin?"

He smiled and said, "Please do."

"What would you like revealed to you from the spirit world?"

"You tell me, my dear, that is why I am here."

My intent would be to do an open reading then. I took out my deck of cards and began to place them on the table after shuffling them; what I saw terrified me. He may be beautiful on the outside, yet, his soul was dark and ugly, at least according to this spread.

I stammered, "Your significator card, the main card is 10; the wheel of fortune. The meaning behind this card is conflicts of interest, unexpected developments, important news that changes or alters your course, also important news, and information. Are you planning any changes in your life?"

"I may be, it all depends . . ."

I did not like his implications or the slight sneer he made when he spoke, ah the devil, a ruv in a man's clothing. He reminded me of a shimulo, preying on the rat of others to survive. I continued, "Next there is 12; the hanged man. This card represents your values and the way you are thinking right now. The way you approach or think about a situation will direct the outcome of the previous card."

He nodded and said, "Continue . . ."

"The Devil, card 15 comes next . . .you will have a negative cycle of events and endure adverse conditions stemming from the choices you make." I began to feel uneasy; I looked up and said to the stranger, "I must end this reading as I do not like to reveal bad news. It is not my place. Please go, there is no charge for this reading."

"No, I insist you finish this."

I pleaded with my eyes to be done and he urged me again, "Please. Continue!"

I was jolted by the force of his words. As I continued my hands began to shake. "Card 16; the tower. Please, I do not wish to . . ."

"Read," he demanded.

"This card reveals unexpected events or devastating conditions, financial problems, separations and divorce conflicts, and loss of one's faith." I thought to myself if any faith exists within this horrible gajo.

"And . . ."

"Card 18; the moon. Inner disturbances, dread, and foreboding. Situations are deceptive . . ."

"It seems my future is not the brightest then?"

"Well, your last card is the star, card 17. This pertains to the future and faith. You may be harmed by harsh words, or circumstances that block your development, it is normally temporary though. Only you can change the outcome. This reading is based on your energy right now, but you have the free-will to change that. If you only ---"

He cut her off. "Maybe I do not want it to change."

I suggested he purchase a bujo, a medicine pouch for his own protection. "I believe that you would benefit from one of these . . ."

"He spat the words, "Gypsy whore, you give me a bad fortune and then you try to take more of my money by tricking me into buying your protection!"

He literally spat on my table and stormed from my ofisa.

I was shaken to the core, but I must continue to work as the day has just begun and now Ganache needed his petalo. This man did not bother to pay her either.

Chapter Six

An hour passed before my next customer entered the tent. It was a kindly older woman who had a beautiful aura. This reading went much better and the woman purchased a bujo as well. The rest of the day was good. I made enough money to hire the ferari and get Ganache back in working order as well as supply my papa with some income. Speaking of Papa, where has the mush gotten off to? I ate a bit of doodah and waited for a while. I went in search of my father as it was dark and tomorrow would be another long day.

I entered an alley way that led to a kertsheema, which is the most likely place to find Papa. I saw a shadow from behind me; I turned and let out a gasp. It was the gajo from my first reading of the day. "Hello, you startled me."

He sneered and said, "I am so sorry, that was not my intention. My intention was to take you by surprise." He laughed a laugh of pure evil.

I turned and tried to flee, but he was upon me in an instant. He grabbed my arm and spun me around. He forced a kiss upon me and forcefully shoved his cheeb into my mouth as I gagged; for that I received a slap to the face!

"Gypsy whore, how dare you refuse me!" He spun me around and shoved me to the ground. He lifted my skirt, tearing my bloomers and forced himself inside of me as I sobbed and begged him to stop. He thrust his karbaro into my mish so hard I felt burning pain, and I cried out.

"Shut up whore, or I will silence you for good!" He put his hand over my mouth and I could barely breathe. I continued to cry, trying to keep my sobs in. He finished and kicked me as he stood to zip his trousers. "Thank you, whore, your cunt is better than your readings, so sweet!" I heard him stride away as I lay there whimpering.

I was able to crawl up against the wall, my balance was off, and I needed to regain my composure. I realized I felt wetness on my thighs; I lifted the edge of my skirts and peered at myself in the dim moonlight. I saw there was blood mixed with his bad seed. I should get home and prepare myself a salve and a tincture quickly before his seed took and I would be carrying his spawn. I tried to stand to no avail. I passed out there where I lay; propped against the building.

Sometime later I was awakened by raucous laughter. As I was blinking my eyes to focus them, I saw my father's muj come into view. He was surrounded by a group of men. "My angel!" He exclaimed. He demanded to know, "Who has done this to you? Kon?"

"Oh, Papa, a gajo wolf, I read for him this morning and I begged him to let me stop as his reading was darkness and nothing more. I foresaw this trouble. He was mean and called me names. He spat on my table as he left. I came looking for you and he caught me here in the alley alone." I began to sob again. Through my tears I murmured he is a shimulo . . ."

"Baby Bear, we shall hunt him down and take care of this. We Natsia stick together."

I begged him and the others, "Please no more bloodshed, Papa, please, I beg of you all."

"We must avenge this injustice. We know how to make him disappear without a trace my love, no one will know."

I whispered, "God will know."

"Come with us my child, you are the only one that can identify him. Which way did he go?"

I pointed up the alley and the men helped me to my feet, my father placed his arm around me for support as we began the search. We found him not far away.

It was my turn to say, "We did not mean to startle you, we wished to take you by surprise!"

With that the men converged on him and I ran away to hide my face. I abhorred violence, even if he deserved it. One mush put his kishti around the shimulo's neck and pulled it tight and they all began to kick him. Once the men beat him to death, my father asked them, "Please take care of the body as I must take my angel home."

The phuro said, "We know of a kasht near here with a deep rebniko. We will row a boat out to the mashakar and weight him down with stones. We will call on the nivasi to bring the fish to eat him. He shall not be found. You have our word. He hugged Claude and they parted ways.

Papa took my vast and said. "Chey, come," and led me back towards camp in the mahala named Quartier Saint Louis. He helped me prepare a bowl to wash myself from. "Thank you, Papa, I can handle it from here. Please rest, tomorrow you must find the ferari and have Ganache's petalo (horse shoe) replaced. I have made enough money to do so and then some. My bujos were a success." I gave a weak smile as he kissed my cheek and entered the vurdon.

I cleansed myself and took a bit of tincture in my tea to ward off pregnancy, although I feared it had been too long to be effective. I could hear the braski and it reminded me of the final resting place of the shimulo. I entered the vardo and crawled into my bed. I was asleep before my head touched the pillow. My sleep was anything but peaceful that night. I had nightmares of the man with the sneer and the assault. *How will I ever tell Marcello?*

Chapter Seven

Upon awakening I felt naswalemos. After lying in bed for another few minutes, I decided to get up and prepare for the day. I would burn some sage to get ready for readings; I felt my body and soul were both soiled. I performed a ceremony and used the sage to smudge myself. I repeated a prayer taught to me by my grandmother:

"I cleanse myself of all selfishness, resentment, critical feeling for my fellow beings, self-condemnation, and misrepresentation of my life experiences. I bathe myself in generosity, appreciation, praise, and gratitude for my fellow beings, self-acceptance, and enlightened understanding of my life experiences."

I love that prayer. My puri daj had shared with me that it came from her friend Lidia Frederico. She had written it and passed it on to her one day after she had been in a bad situation. Hopefully it was not as bad of a situation as had occurred last night. This will be one of those experiences that hang over me for a long time to come, and I may need more than sage and prayers to forget and forgive.

I went out to the campfire to prepare breakfast. I took the skillet from the side of the wagon and added some butter to it, stoking the fire while the pan heated. I first cooked the sausage to give the pan a good greasing and then broke a few eggs into the pan, adding chives, and some fromage cheese into the mixture. I scrambled them together. I took a few pieces of the pressed bread to add on the side. After the food was done, I removed the kettle from the fire and made myself a nice tisane.

I called for father. "Papa, breakfast is ready. Opre!"

I heard an unintelligible grunt from adre the vardo. I wrapped up his food and sat it inside, near him so he would see it when he awoke. I looked at myself in my small mirror and decided today I would wear a dicklo, the head scarf of a married woman, so I do not have the same trouble which occurred yesterday. I entered my fortune telling tent and prepared it for the customers.

My first customer arrived an hour after I opened the bolta. It was a tall, thin, striking woman with dark hair and emerald eyes. She looked as if she came from barvalimos. She inquired about a reading and then asked, "What are all of the plants hanging around you and what are those strange pouches used for?"

I explained the purpose of the pouches and herbs adding, "I can customize one for your needs, Madame."

She looked pensive and then spoke. "I believe I might like one, but first would you be so kind as to tell my fortune?"

"Do you have a question in mind?'

"Well, as a matter of fact, I do. My louse of a husband did not come home again last night. He makes a habit out of it; not coming home, that is. I would like to know if you can tell me where he was last night."

"I am sorry I am not able to be so specific, but I can tell you if it is in your best interest to stay with him."

"Okay then, how does this work?"

Please place your hands on the crystal ball beside mine, so they are touching. I will ask your permission to tap into your thoughts, your energy, which is connected to his, and see what I am shown." We proceeded to put our hands on the ball and I began to chant.

In no time, I was in a trance state and I saw the woman's husband clearly in my mind's eye. I let out an audible gasp.

"What, what have you seen?"

"I am sorry, I saw a shadowy figure, and it seemed to want to do harm. Forgive me for gasping, it took me unawares."

"The woman looked aghast and said, "It wishes to harm whom?"

"I am sorry Madame; I broke the connection when I gasped. If you will allow me, I will tap back into your field."

The woman gave her consent.

"I see a man, he is quite good looking, he is tall and his lip lifts a bit on one side when he smiles . . ."

The woman leaned closer, "Yes, yes, that sounds like my husband."

"He is out late and this shadow figure, it is stalking him. I feel he may be in danger."

The woman looked Crystobella in the eye and said, "I hope it gets him, he is a scoundrel!"

I was shocked at her disdain for her own husband. Yet, I understood her completely, because the man I saw was the man who had attacked me last night. I went on, "I feel that he is not a good match for you. You feel quite stuck with him and he brings you much sorrow."

"Yes, he does bring me sorrow. I thought he loved me, but I fear he loved my money more, and he loves to be in the company of whores as well. I feel embarrassed. The entire town snickers behind my back. Now you know why I hope the shadow man gets him."

"Madame, I am so sorry. Shall we continue and see what your future holds?"

"Please, go on."

"I see happiness and joy entering your life. You will meet someone new in a year's time and they will adore you, it will be all you have ever hoped for."

"That is splendid news, but what do I do about him, the scoundrel?"

"I am unable to advise you as to that Madame, perhaps a divorce?"

"I could not bear to be ridiculed and talked about, it is bad enough they do it now, but if I publicly declare him a cad . . . well I shan't."

"Possibly it will work itself out Madame."

"Please dear, call me Adrienne; I am Adrienne Gabriel-Jacques'."

I extended my hand, "Pleased to make your acquaintance, you may call me Crystobella."

She shook my hand and said, "likewise, my dear."

I handed her a small jade stone for protection. "It is a gift; it offers you protection from negative forces. It shall shield you from harm and increase love, it brings the wearer harmony."

"Thank you my dear, I shall have it made into a pendant. Now may I have one of your special pouches filled with your magical herbs?"

"I do not create magick; I just understand medicinal uses of plants and how they can offer gifts to the person who holds them sacred."

"Well I know I can use some of those gifts. What do I owe you for your services?"

"Twelve deniers or one sol please."

Adrienne gave me a livre, saying, "You may keep the change, dear child."

"I rarely get paid so much for my gifts, thank you."

The woman then took my hand and slipped an ècu into it. "This is for you and you alone my dear. Keep it safe for a rainy day." And she was gone before I looked back up from looking at my palm.

I was so shocked to see his face when I looked into her soul. The poor woman may have wealth, yet, she lacked the love she craved. I pray she did not suspect us of anything.

Adrienne must have given me a good word as I had many women of status come to see me that day. Just as I was getting ready to close my tent a man approached me.

I turned and smiled at him, "How may I help you, sir?"

He introduced himself as Constable Caron. "I am looking into the disappearance of a man named Delano Jacques'. I was informed he was seen around your tent yesterday morning."

"I see many people constable, can you describe him please?" I remained calm and collected, yet, I was terrified he could see inside my head, that he somehow knew what we had done. I smiled again at him to encourage him to give me the man's description.

He made a point of looking at his notes, "Well, he is about one meter, eighty-five centimeters tall, he has blue eyes and sandy brown hair, most women describe him as handsome." He looked up at her expectantly.

"I do recall a handsome gentleman who came to see me yesterday morning. He left soon after he sat down at my table. It seems he was not happy with his fortune; I offered him a refund. He spit on the ground before he got up to leave. I hope he has not done anything untoward, should I be frightened?"

"Oh, no, miss. You misunderstand. He is missing, as in he never came home last night or today. He has been gone over twenty-four hours now and his wife is worried. Normally, we would wait a few more days before conducting an inquiry, but they are aristocrats."

"I see; I am sorry I cannot be of more help."

"It is all right, miss. Thank you for your help."

"Certainly constable. Have a nice evening."

He tipped his hat at me as he turned to leave. I was able to breathe again now that he was gone. I must warn my father that there was inquiry. I felt sure that Adrienne was just playing the part of the worried wife; she must be secretly overjoyed at his disappearance.

Tonight, I would not make the mistake of venturing out to look for my father; Claude would roll in sooner or later. I needed some sustenance and rest. I was still bleeding and not feeling well. At least tomorrow we could head back home. Hopefully that was Papa's plan. I must speak with Marcello soon. I miss him and need to feel his strong arms around me, protecting and comforting me.

Chapter Eight

Claude came in during the wee hours of the morning once more. He stumbled and fell as he came in the doorway waking me. "Papa, is that you?"

"Yes, my Ba . . . Bab . . . Baby Bear," he said slurring his words.

"Oh, Papa, drunk again?"

"Schuh- ish, Bear, I will sleep it off."

"Good, Papa, but first tell me do we leave today?"

"No Angel . . ."

I could only hear his snoring and knew that I would get no more answers until late afternoon. It shall be up to me to find the ferari and get Ganache's shoe put on. I covered my shera in a dicklo again, just for protection from rude comments, if not worse. I found the ferari in a stable near the Palace of Versailles. He was also of Gypsy descent. I addressed him in Romane, "Bonjour, sar san Kako?"

"Sastimos schej."

"Kako, my grai is in need of a petalo. I have the money to pay. Can you help me?"

"Yes, can you bring him to me?"

"I was hoping you could come to us. I have a pair and the mare is younger. She may create a ruckus if I leave her. We are camped by the market place in the Quartier San Louis."

"It is difficult to come with all of my tools and I will need the fire to be hot to shape the shoe."

"Yes, of course, I shall fetch them then." I began to leave and turned back toward him "Could you possibly help by assisting me and leading the mare?"

He grunted but closed up his barn and came along with me. We arrived and I handed him the lead for Madeleine. He said "My, she is baro for a mare!"

"Aye, she is. She is a dya; in foal to Ganache here. They shall have a fine foal.

"Yes, they are a nice pair; the offspring should be barri and zor."

We led the pair back to his barn. He made the petalo and fit it to Ganache's hoof perfectly. "Lead him so I may see him ga."

I did as I was instructed. I took him away from the ferari and returned toward him.

"Good, his ga is straight and his stride is well."

"What do I owe you kako?'

"With the price of the petalo, it shall be one livrè."

I handed him the coin and asked, "Would you be so kind as to help me get the pair back, please?"

He went through the grumbling and barn closing once more and then took the mare's lead rope. "Let's go rakli, I don't have all day. Time is money, my dear."

We exchanged pleasantries as we walked. He asked her, "Did you hear an aristocrat has gone missing?"

"Yes, the shanglo came to see me yesterday. I guess the man had visited me in the morning for a reading, yet, I did not know who he was or that he had gone missing until Constable Caron told me so."

"I knew of him; he and his wife are the talk of the town. I bet he ran off with one of his hussies. He likes the ladies, he does."

"All I know is that he is a vile gajo and I want never to encounter him again."

"Yes, good riddance, I say as well."

I took the lead rope from him and thanked him again for his work. Then bid him a good afternoon, Bon après-midi, kako."

I was happy that no one was that concerned with the disappearance of the shimulo. The whole village must believe he ran off with another woman. I felt sorry for Adrienne. Yet, knew it was the best thing for her, saving her the embarrassment of a divorce. I must wake Papa and speak with him. The sooner we are away from the town the better. Sooner or later people may connect us to him. Although, it would not be one of their Natsia, they would adhere to the Gypsy laws.

I made sure the horses were taken care of and entered the wagon. I shook my father gently by the shoulder. "Opre! Papa, I must speak with you."

He moaned and turned over, I tried again, "Papa, we must speak. The shanglo came today."

At that word he rolled over and opened his eyes "What? Who came by?"

"The constable, Papa."

"Did he say what he was looking for?"

"Yes, he was looking into the disappearance of that awful gajo."

"What did you tell him, my Baby Bear?"

"I told him the tachiben, Papa; that he was here in the morning and was not happy with his fortune, so he left."

"Did he act as if he suspected something?"

"No, I think it is because he cheats on his wife, the entire town knows and the ferari told me everyone thinks he ran off with a whore."

"The ferari, did you fetch him yourself, Baby Bear?"

"Yes, Papa, we must be leaving soon."

"If we leave now, we shall draw suspicion. If we leave tomorrow it will look normal. Don't worry my angel, no one will ever find him. His wife and this towne are better off without him."

"I know father, yet I wish to put this place behind me, I never wish to return here. For me, it holds bad memories and lashav.

"You have no reason to hold shame, my dear one. He is the monster. You were his victim. You shall hold yourself proud, this will be forgotten soon. Now, where is my dinner?"

"It is here, Papa; well it was your breakfast. I can heat it up for you if you'd like."

"I would like that very much, Baby Bear."

I took his plate to the fire so I could fulfill his wish. I returned in a few moments with the plate; "Here you are, Papa. It is tato, Sastimos, enjoy."

"Thank you."

I realized my stomach was grumbling and decided to cook myself something to eat. My father had brought home a hare, I decided to clean it and make xaimoko, that would feed us for a few days and he will be hungry later, this will be good with his beloved herb bread, of which I ate some to allow the grumbling to subside. I skinned and cleaned the rabbit, placing it on a spit to cook over the open flame. I began to cut the vegetables, dropping them in the large stew pot with the boiling water; the smell of the herbs was floating aromatically on the breeze. I enjoyed cooking; it took my mind off of my worries. Once the meat was cooked, I added it to the pot and covered it with the lid to simmer for a few hours.

I checked on Papa, but he must have slipped out of the back door of the vurdon, he was off to engage in shenanigans again. I rolled an herbal cigarette and sat down to enjoy my smoke. I wondered where the mulla was. Most likely he was eaten by swine or some other such fate, possibly in a swamp. There was one near where they left the Natsia. That is why I heard the frogs. Wherever it was, I hope his dark soul stayed with the corpse.

Chapter Nine

I loved to visit the royal garden and decided to take a stroll, it was over by the river, and it was one of the loveliest places I have ever been to. I strolled in the gardens at the Place d'Armes, marveling at the topiary and fountains, but traversing the labyrinths is my favorite thing to do. It is like a meditation for me. I always say a prayer when I come to the center of the maze.

I was walking back to the camp when I saw the vegetables at Le Potager du Roi, it is the king's royal vegetable garden, and they sell the extra in a stall by the entrance. I purchased some tomatoes and lettuce, I would make a salad to go with our rabbit stew, and I may purchase some fresh bogacha; I tire of the compressed bread sometimes.

Just before camp I saw the Versailles Cathedral, I stepped inside. I went to the altar and crossed myself. I was not a religious person. Yet, I often did this, possibly it came from another lifetime. I said a prayer for the muller'd gajo. I prayed for his mule to be set free. I silently feared his mulani would haunt us. Death was not always the end of torment for a soul or for the living which it felt vengeance toward. I added prayers for my father, the men that helped him, and for myself. I left a denier in the small donation box and lit a candle for all involved in the narky business. I hurried to the campsite. It was time to tend the horses.

I fed them and made sure they had plenty of straw to keep them dry and comfortable in the night. The kham was setting and it was a beautiful display. I rolled another cigarette and began to daydream as I smoked it. My mind was a million miles away when my father interrupted my musings.

"Baby Bear, I am home."

"Oh, Papa, you have returned early tonight."

He said, "Yes, my dear one, I decided to stay close to camp tonight, I do not want to draw attention to myself as I overheard the townsfolk saying the shanglo was looking to lel those responsible for the disappearance of the gajo. They say there is no evidence of a crime, yet, the man paid the constable well to look the other way when he was on the prowl. The constable shall not like losing his extra love. It is best we jil avree. But tonight, we dance!" He pulled out his lavuta and began to play.

A Didikai of mine came over from the Kumpania to join in the fun, soon after her familia joined her. We danced around the fire and shared a drink made from wine and herbs. I felt so happy and so tipsy, but could not stop dancing. The other women and I were lifting our skirts and dancing around the yog vigorously. We were singing and the men were playing various instruments. I had not danced like this since my puri daj passed. The vista gathered and had a celebration of life for my puri daj; she was beloved by all that knew her! Beautiful Rosa lee.

It was almost sunrise when the party ended. I was never so happy to get into my bed. Sov overtook me at once. I dreamt of Marcello. He and I were living together in his cottage. I was in the garden and when I stood up, I was with Chahvi. He came up from behind me and wrapped his arms around me. I felt his love and the child growing adre of me. I had on a lovely vezlime' dress. I knew it was a gift from my beloved. I was in love with life . . . The tato of the day was stifling and it tore me from my dream world. The vurdon was like a bov; I opened the doors and windows. I looked out and saw the kham was high in the sky; we slept through the morning and into the day.

"Papa, Papa, opre! Wake up. We must get on the road. Papa!"

"Chey! Please be quiet!"

"Papa, it is late, we must go. It is hot today; the horses will need many breaks. After all Madeleine is in foal. Papa, opre! up!"

"All right! I am up, now please stop yelling; my head is pounding."

I told him, "I have some fresh bogacha and gooi. I shall fetch it for you." I returned and handed him his bowl and a nice kafa.

"Thank you, my angel."

"I will hitch up the team Papa, and you can drive, it is time to be on our drom."

"Mon chèri, I will drive all day if you wish."

"Thank you, Papa."

When we were on our way, I reminded him, "I need to look for my bujo, Papa. You said we could, remember?"

"Baby Bear, I feel that in light of the events which occurred in Versailles, we should avoid trouble at all costs, don't you agree?"

"Papa, I do but I treasure my bujo so much, I beg of you to let me stop."

"Okay, but at the first sign of trouble we shall leave, do you agree, mon chèri?"

"Yes, Papa, I agree. Why are you calling me mon chèri?"

"Just something I picked up in Versailles." He winked at me.

"If you are lucky, that is all you picked up in the brothels, Papa."

Chapter Ten

We rode in silence until we arrived at the small village. The same man was at the roadside stand. Claude stopped the wagon. I got down, "Baby Bear, allow your papa to handle this . . ."

"I can handle this, Papa." I approached the man, and held out my hand that had an ècu in it, and before he could snatch it, I closed my palm. This is yours in exchange for the small pouch I dropped last time I was here. I saw you pick it up."

He spat on the ground, "Yes, I did pick it up, and it had no money in it!"

"Well, it is just a draba, a charm, I would like it back, it holds no value for you, but this coin does."

He thought about it for a few moments while he scratched his chin. "I still have it; it is behind the stand on the shelf. I will trade you, but I want two ècu."

"I only have one; I can add a sol if that would do?" I reached into my potchee and added the sol.

He said, "It is better than the herbs and button which are in your pouch." He went behind the stand and returned with my pouch. He handed it to me as I dropped the coins into his hand.

"Thank you, sir; I bid you a good day." I backed up to the wagon.

"Papa, we can go now," I said as I climbed onto the buckboard. I had forgotten about my puri daj's kocho, I was glad to have it back.

He clucked and told the horses to giddy-up. I hugged him and gave him a kiss on the cheek. "Thank you so much, Papa."

It was well after dark when we arrived at our home Kumpania. "Crystobella, will you tend to the horses?"

"Yes, Papa, I will,"

"I will visit a didikai, a rawnie, don't wait up, Baby Bear."

"I never do, Papa, have fun."

I wished it was not so late, I needed to see my beloved Marcello. I got the horses bedded down and lit the yog, making sure it was stoked well koshter to move the coals around and fueled it to last until morning. Right now, I needed to lie down and enjoy the tablipen the yog was giving off. I grabbed a perina and laid it on the ground beside the fire. I lay upon the blanket and looked to the stars. They were so beautiful, I felt as if I was floating among them and I dozed off.

I was awakened by a hand over my mouth. I struggled to free myself. Then I heard Marcello's voice. "Mi amor, I have been waiting in the tree line for you to arrive. I did not want to take a chance on anyone seeing us; I waited until your father left and the neighbors were gone to their beds. I have missed you." He said, "We should go inside the wagon so as not to be discovered."

I used a nickname for him. "Oh, veshengo, if Papa comes back, he will kill you!"

"I saw your father go to the wagon of the towne whore, he had another woman on one arm and a bottle in his hand, with two women and a full bottle of spirits, I should think you will not see him until tomorrow afternoon."

I led him to the vardo, I said, we need to speak, but first I must have you near me. I removed my dress and unbuttoned his shirt, pressing my berk against his chest, I worked at his zipper.

He said, "Let me help you, mi amor." And he removed his trousers.

We lay on my bed, and the moonlight illuminated my bronzed skin, as he bent over me, he suckled first one breast and then the other. He slid his hand between my legs; I made a small whimpering sound. "What is it my love?"

"I must tell you the truth. I have been marime by a vile man. He raped me and I am hurt, down there. I shall understand if you no longer want me." I hung my head and began to weep.

"Marcello took my chin in his hand and tilted my face toward his, he kissed me ever so gently. "I will love you no matter what, do you not understand this?"

I clung to him saying, "I love you more than life itself, Marcello, I always will."

"Let's get dressed and I will hold you tonight, there will be plenty of time for our lovemaking. Tonight, I want you to feel safe."

We slept in one another's arms until daybreak, "I must slip away, mi amor. Can you come to me this afternoon?"

"Yes, my beloved, I will come to you."

He kissed me and was gelo like a Kesali. I got up and took care of the horses.

Chapter Eleven

Claude did not come home until later in the afternoon. I decided to confront him about his philandering ways. "Papa, I must speak with you about something."

"What is it, Baby Bear?"

"I would like to know where you were all night and most of this day?"

"My angel, that is not for you to worry about."

"I think it is, Papa, you expect me to work and take care of everything while you are out philandering and drinking away the earnings. I feel as if I am your slave at times. Although, I know you love me, I feel you need to be more responsible and help me with chores."

"I think that we do okay. You have a roof over your head and a full stomach. Why should my social activities bother you?"

"Papa, I was left here alone all night, I am not able to defend myself if an intruder was to happen upon our camp, and after the attack in Versailles . . . I am feeling vulnerable."

"Come to me, my child." I walked to him and he embraced me. "I love you, Baby Bear. I do not mean to make you feel vulnerable. I sometimes behave selfishly, yes, but I have needs . . . since your mother died, I have been alone and . . ."

"Papa, I understand you have needs, I am just asking for you to be a bit more responsible where drinking and women are concerned, please."

"Yes, my dear. Now what is for dinner?"

I rolled my eyes and gave an exasperated sigh. "In one ear and out of the other! I will get the stew heated up for you, Papa." I prepared his food and told him I needed to go in search of some herbs and mushrooms in the waver."

"Be careful Angel, I shall see you later this evening then?"

"Yes, Papa, I shall be home before dark."

I made my way along the path in the kasht until I was out of my father's sight. Then I darted into the waver and weaved a path to Marcello's cottage. I tapped on his door. He opened the door almost immediately.

"Mi amor!" He picked me up and spun me around, before gently putting me down inside the door and closing it.

"Marcello, I am so glad to see you, my love!"

"I have missed you my darling. I have been experiencing some light seizures the past week and I am in need of your tincture."

I slipped a small vial from my posoti and handed it to him. "Here, my love, this will ease the effects of your seizures. I shall also give you a therapeutic massage."

"I like the sound of that, amor." He planted a passionate kiss on my lips.

"I said therapeutic!" She giggled. "Now, get undressed and lie down on your bed please."

"I love a woman who takes charge of a situation!" He teased. He did as I told him and lay down on the bed.

I draped a sheet over his buttocks and poured some of my special oil on his back. It had drarnego in it. I began to chant a song while I rubbed his back. When I finished, I moved to his feet and began to pray and channel energy from Devel, the creator, through me and into him. I finished with a cranial sacral massage, easing the tension in his head. "There you are, my love. Your seizures should abate now, please take your tincture morning and evening for the best results." After you are dressed, join me in the kitchen for a tisane."

He dressed and came into the kitchen and sat down. "Mi amor, I wish to be your husband, I cannot wait; it is torture having to meet in secret. Please let us go and elope."

"Marcello, you know my father would not allow it, he would take me and flee in the night; I am after all, his bread and butter, literally and figuratively. I would never see you again, and I would rather die than endure that fate. My love, I must ask a favor of you. "

"Anything for you Angel."

"Can you make me a wooden box with a false bottom where I can safely keep the drawings my grandmother gave me? You know we have superstitions. I am not supposed to have any of my grandmother's property. We do this to keep the person's Mulani from haunting us. It was to be destroyed upon her death. Yet, she secreted the family drawings and a healing pouch, a bujo, to me. Papa knows of the pouch as I lost it on our travels and I had to beg him to return to the place so I could retrieve it. But he would destroy the drawings if he saw them, he misses my mother so much that it has driven him to drink, and I think seeing her likeness would drive him mad."

"Of course, I shall have it ready by next week, my love. Now how about some attention? Come sit in my lap."

I did as he requested. "I have missed you so and I yearn to experience jekhipe with you, but I fear I am still tender, but we can try my love, I have brought an oil to help lubricate the area."

His eyes began to twinkle and he hoisted me into his arms and carried me to the bedroom once more. He laid me on the bed ever so gently. He carefully removed my clothing and then removed his own. He began to massage me with the oil, gradually moving into my private areas, using his fingers to moisten my flower, at first, I flinched slightly.

"Amor, is it okay?"

"Yes, my love, just be gentle with me, have patience."

"Yes, my darling." *The sensual act was arousing him to the point of surrender, yet, he pushed his need for her down and kept gently preparing her for his entry. When she began to whimper with need, he climbed above her and covered her, inching himself inside of her with the gentleness of a lamb. She moved under him with a slow grinding motion and he met her motion with his own. He began to kiss her; dipping his tongue in and out of her mouth, her sweet, pink mouth. He stiffened and succumbed to his release.*

We climaxed as one and I murmured … "Yekhipe."

Marcello pleaded with me, "Yes, we are one, we will always be one, for eternity. I am yours and you are mine, please, mi amor, become my wife?"

"Oh, Marcello, I just explained why this cannot come to pass, at least right now. Maybe later when I am older . . ."

He rolled off of me and replied, "I know, I want you every day to be with me."

"I must go now; my father thinks I am gathering herbs and mushrooms. If I am to be home before dark, I must gather some, so he does not become suspicious." I dressed and kissed him on the cheek while reaching for the door. "Goodbye, my sweet lover, my love, my life, until we meet again."

As I walked through the doorway, he grabbed me around the waist, spinning me around and kissed me passionately once more, then playfully patted my bottom and pushed me out the door. "Goodbye, mi amor."

I was searching for herbs and realized the kham was beginning to dip low in the sky, I felt uneasy, as if there was a mule watching me. A small creature scurried from behind a bush, startling me and I thought; *I must be jittery, I am now letting small animals scare me and imagining ghosts following me. I need to settle myself.*

I said a small prayer. "From this day forward, I shall condemn the thoughts the dark side sends to penetrate my mind and declare that I will defeat the darkness, the light lives within me and where the light dwelleth nothing else may enter. Amen."

I found a few mushrooms and added them to the basket hurrying home; I still could not be rid of the feeling of a negative force hanging over me. I saw my father was home sitting in a chair, stoking the fire, and smoking a cigarette. "May I join you, Papa?"

"Please, Baby Bear, sit."

I pulled up a chair and began to roll my own herbal cigarette. I finished and my father lit it for me. I inhaled its rich herbal mixture, feeling a sense of calm settle over me. I decided to share with my father the sense of foreboding I felt in the waver. "Papa, while I was in the woods, I felt this sense of something ominous following me, a mule, or worse. I could not rid it, no matter how much I prayed or believed in the light."

"Angel, you let darane svatura fuel your thoughts. You must not dwell on such nonsense."

"Papa, there are supernatural forces which influence the living, it is not nonsense."

"You sound just like your dya and puri daj! That is all they ever spoke of!"

"Papa, please believe me, I feel that the shimulo who we muller'd has not left the earth plane and he intends to do us harm . . . please, Papa, I beg you to listen."

"Baby Bear, why don't you make a special protection pouch for you and one for me, you put so much faith in your bujos, then believe in your medicine, your magic."

"You are correct father; I shall make us both bujos in the morning, for protection. I think that we should acquire a large rikono as well, he will alert us to intruders."

"Baby Bear, how will a rikono ward off a mulani?"

"One never knows, Papa, one never knows. I just know I would feel safer with a rikono to guard camp."

"Okay, you may acquire a dog."

"I will head to the market tomorrow to find the perfect one! Thank you, Papa, I love you." I kissed him on the top of the head and went the vardo. I still felt uneasy and decided to do a house cleansing to be safe. I lit the herbs and incanted a prayer. *"Negative energy may not stay. I release it and send it on its way. Negative energy I banish thee and is my word so mote it be!"*

I made a snack of cheese, some compressed bread, and wine. I carried it out to my father. "Here Papa, I have brought a snack for us to share. It is nice to spend the evening with you and enjoy the yog." I poured him some wine and handed him the glass, setting the plate between us on the small table adorned with scarves.

"Thank you, Baby Bear."

We enjoyed the food and then smoked another cigarette together. We pi a few more glasses of wine and I began to feel tired. "Papa, I must retire now. Will I see you in the morning?"

"Yes, Baby Bear, I shall stay with you tonight."

I checked the horses and noticed they were skittish. I sang softly to them while stroking them trying to ease their fear. "My ponies, it is okay, rest now and tomorrow we will have our new guard dog, our protector."

I headed to my bed. I slept fitfully once more. My dreams were filled with the sneering face of my attacker. He grabbed me and threw me to the ground, again penetrating me with such force I felt as if I would break in two. I cried out in my sleep and awoke. My father was there and he stirred in his sleep, but did not awaken. I began to weep quietly in my bed. I felt the presence with me still. I could not get away from it. It meant to do me harm, of that I was sure. Eventually I fell back to sleep and awoke when I felt the sunbeams warming the wagon. I stretched and saw that Papa was still asleep, so I crept silently from the vurdon.

I greeted my horses; giving each one a kiss and blowing into their nostrils, it is the greeting that they do to one another as their olfactory glands never forget a scent and they can tell friend from foe in this manner. Madeleine snorted when I approached her. "What is it girl, are you okay?"

I stroked the mare and calmed her. I felt the presence again. "Ah, it is the mule, isn't It, girl. It is okay, I shall deal with it." I kissed them and threw them some hay. It was time to prepare breakfast and get to the market.

I added wood to the fire and after eating I remembered that I needed to make the bujos for myself and my father. I better make one for Marcello to be safe, after all he is as much a part of my life as my father and the Mulani may attack him as well.

I left my father's plate of food and his bujo on the table by his bed. I also left a note telling him I would be at the market and would return to make him his dinner. I whistled a lovely tune my mother had taught me as I strolled to the market. When I arrived, I went to the place the locals called puppy alley. This is where I shall find my protector.

I went to each stall, inspecting its occupants closely. I narrowed down my choices to the Dogue de Bordeaux, a fierce looking stocky breed. The breeder told me about the dog's history: "Powerful and muscular, this French breed is a molossiod, which means it is a mastiff-type dog. They have a massive head and a stocky body, the history of the Dogue de Bordeaux is shrouded in mystery. Different theories link the breed to the Bull mastiff, Bulldog, and Tibetan Mastiff, but it was undisputedly descended from ancient breeding stock and has been used as a guardian and hunter for centuries. Trained to hunt boar, herd cattle, and protect the homes of their masters they are excellent guard dogs."

I inquired, "What is the price of this fine dog?"

"This fine dog requires the price of twelve livres, or a demi-louis gold coin. They are the crème de la crème, after all."

"I shall look at the rest of the lot and let you know my choice." Thank you for showing me your fine dogs."

"You are a Gypsy girl, no? You cannot afford my dogs."

"Sir, I can afford your dogs, I do work for a living. I may not be the crème de la crème of society, but I believe in paying a fair price for a quality dog. I believe your dog is worth the price, I must look at all of the dogs to be fair to them as well, as the one who touches my soul, and calls to me is the one that is to be mine."

"Ah, you Gypsies are a kooky lot!"

"Good day, sir."

I was glad that I kept my composure with that rude man, and equally glad that none of his dogs called to me. It was not the dogs' faults after all, but I did not want to give that mean man one denier of my hard-earned money."

I looked at Great Pyranese and the Pyrean Shepherd, yet, none of them held my fancy. The next stall held a breed called Beuceron. I felt this was the stall; my soul mate in dog form resided here, I could feel it. I peered over the edge of the stall and I saw a shy, quiet one curled up in the corner. The rest of the litter where pawing and clawing the sides of the stall, vying for my attention, but that one, he called to my heart, to my soul. I whistled softly and he looked up, meeting my gaze with his, as if he had been waiting for me. I asked the breeder, "May I see that one; the one in the corner?"

"Aye, miss, that one is an odd one, he is. I shall sell him to you for half-price if you like him. He reached over the edge and grabbed the pup, it yelped as he hauled it out of the stall. He handed it to me and I held him close peering into his face. He licked my face and snuggled closer. I knew this was our new guardian. "I shall take him. What is his price?"

The man said, "Normally he would be the same price as the rest of 'em, an ècu, but you can have him for three livers. Or sixty sol if you like, whichever you have."

She reached into her katrinsa potchee and produced the required fee for the pooch. The man looked surprised that I had the amount needed. I said "Thank you, sir. He shall have a good home. Good day to you."

The man tipped his hat and I hugged my boy close to my chest and sang to him as I walked away, I curtseyed to the man with the Dogue de Bordeaux's and he spat on the ground as I passed. I despised rudeness and thought that man deserved to lose a sale with his poor attitude. But, even so, that stall did not hold my dog. I had found the perfect one! Now what to call him. I loved that he was streyino.

All the way home I thought about a name for him. I finally decided on Beauregard, after all, he had the word Beau in his name, so his nickname Beau would suit him fine and Beauregard was a fine name for a protector. In France the name Beauregard means respected, regarded highly, and a handsome gaze. This fit him perfectly.

I was excited to show my father, but he was not at camp when I returned. I showed the horses their new protector; they snorted and sniffed the pup, the pup played with them pouncing on the nose of Ganache, making him jump. I laughed at their antics. I made a small bed for my baby, so he could sleep next to me inside the vurdon, at least until he was grown.

My father returned in the late afternoon. He saw me playing with the puppy. He approached me. "Who do we have here?"

"Papa, I would like you to meet Beauregard, or Beau for short. He is a handsome specimen of a guard dog. He called to my soul. He shall be our protector."

"Dear daughter, have you not noticed he is a small puppy?"

"Of course, I have, Papa. He will grow to be big and strong. He was the odd one of the litter and the man gave him to me for half the price. I believe he was made to be my protector. He is perfect."

"If you say so, Baby Bear, he is a cute little fellow."

"His father is grand. They are tall and strong dogs yet lean. They were bred to be herding dogs and have been around since the fifteen-hundreds. They are tireless and are good at guarding flocks, herds, and households. He will weigh around forty livres when he is full grown. I love his tan and black color, he looks regal, yet rough around the edges. He is perfect, Papa, is he not?"

"He is perfect, my angel. I am glad you have your protector. Now what is for dinner?"

"Goose, Papa, I picked up a bit of popin-mas at the market and a few vegetables for your supper. It is cooking on the fire now. It shall be ready soon."

"I hope so child, I am starving."

"What were you out doing, Papa?'

"I was working, I decided to be useful, as you suggested. I got a job on a team building a barn, a stanya."

"Papa!" I exclaimed, "I am so proud of you!" I ran to him and gave him a hug. "Did you find your bujo and food by your bedside today?"

"Yes, Baby Bear, I did. Thank you, I kept it in my pocket all day. And it shall be near me always."

I prepared the dinner for him, sneaking a bit of mas to the new pup. He licked my fingers and it tickled. I could not wait to show Marcello my puppy! It would have to wait until tomorrow when Papa was at work. I tried to telepathically let Marce' know I would be there tomorrow. I felt it was possible for us to communicate this way as we are as one on this plane and in the spirit realm. I knew him before this life and I am certain I shall know him after this life as well.

My father ate with me by the fire. We rolled and smoked together once more. He asked me, "Will you be working at the market this week?"

"I am going to sell my herbs and tisanes on Wednesday, Papa. I will be doing readings on the weekend at the Reveler's Faire. I think the cirque will return next month as well. I can work daily there for the month that it is in towne."

"This is all good news, Baby Bear. I am glad we are both being productive."

"Yes, Papa, it is a good thing."

"Maybe you will find a nice young manus at the cirque?"

"Oh, Papa, not this again, please. I have told you I have a suitor, if you would just try to get to know him, I am sure you would love him . . ."

"Angel, maw! You are to marry within your Natsia. I shall not waiver on this. There are many fine young men to choose from within our nation, you must carry on a nav-romano."

"Yes, Papa." It did me no good to mang. It was best if I just conceded and let him think he has won this battle. I vowed to Devel that nothing on this earth shall keep me from Marcello.

Chapter Twelve

The next morning after my father left for work, I headed to Marcello's, still keeping to the roundabout way to cover my tracks, the small pup following on my heels. I still felt the presence of the mule. I knew it was a prikasa. When I arrived at Marcello's door, I tapped lightly, and he answered at once.

"Mi amor!" He grabbed me and pulled me in nearly shutting Beau in the door.

"Wait," I exclaimed. "My puppy!"

He looked down and indeed there was a puppy at her feet. It looked up at him with its tongue hanging out to one side and appeared to be grinning at him. "Who is this fine little fellow?"

"It is my new protector and guardian, Beauregard!" I smiled broadly.

"I love him." He bent down and scooped Beau up into his arms. He talked to him in a soothing manner and took him to the kitchen for a bit of meat.

"He is getting spoiled eating so well. Papa does not know I sneak him meat from our stock."

He placed the pup on the floor and we sat down and played with him for a bit. Marcello tied one of his old socks in a knot and played tug-o-war with the puppy. He released the sock and Beau tumbled over backward, this made me laugh with delight.

I gave Marcello the bujo I had made for him and asked him to keep it close to his heart. I told him of the strange feeling I have had as of late and my suspicions of it being the man from Versailles. I said, "We have done a terrible thing, Marcello. I do not believe that one person has the right to take the life another, no matter what trespasses they have committed."

Marcello said, "You did nothing, mi amor."

"He is a mule, a mulani, he is haunting me. I feel his awful energy around me and it has been spooking my horses as well."

"Now, now, mi amor, I shall protect you."

"Marcello, I beg of you please wear your bujo."

"I will mi amor."

"Shall we retire to your bed, my love; I shall enjoy another tryst before I go home to prepare for tomorrow's market."

We went to the bedroom and made love; I liked how gentle he was with me, but at times wished he could be more aggressive, I told him so. "Marce' pull my hair and come into me from behind . . ."

He moved behind her, wrapping her glorious hair around his hand and giving it a firm tug as he slipped inside of her as they stood on their knees. She bent her head back and bit her bottom lip, he could not help himself and bent down and bit her neck gently.

I gasped and begged him for komi and he began to thrust harder and I fell forward onto my hands and knees, as he pounded me harder and harder until I felt his seed flowing within me. I fell to the bed and he on top of me.

I loved to feel his weight on top of me, and it was comforting. We rolled together so he was facing up and then embraced. Both of us dozing off until the barking of the pup woke us.

There was a knock on the door. Marcello grabbed his clothes and hurriedly dressed and answered his door. He was shocked to see Claude standing on his door stoop. He hoped Crystobella heard his voice and hid with her pup, keeping him quiet. Dying was not on his calendar today. "How can I help you Mr. Franco?"

"My daughter has told me you are a fine carpenter, and your reputation precedes you, when I asked for a carpenter everyone in town assured me you were the man to see. We need your help on the barn we are building in the towne."

"I would be glad to come and give my assistance. When shall I be there?"

"Tomorrow morning will be fine, at seven if you can."

"I will be there promptly, Claude, thank you for offering me the job."

He closed the door and waited a few moments before returning to his room. He found Crystobella under the bed, covered in dust; clutching the pup and holding its little nose and mouth so he could not bark. "You can come out now, my little dust mouse."

"Is he gone?"

"Yes, mi amor. I do not think he suspects us. Do not worry." He dusted the cobwebs from her hair and gave her a kiss, now you should go and get back before he finds you gone, take your short-cut."

I carried the pup as I ran through the woods; I made it home just moments before Papa. He came up to give me a hug; "My angel, why are you flushed?"

"Papa, I was in the wood and I felt that presence again, it scares me, so I ran back here, I know that mule is after us, after me!" I began to cry.

"It is okay, I think it is your guilt creating this fear. You did nothing, my angel, nothing, do you understand this?"

"Yes, Papa, I know, but we should have let the police arrest him and have a jury decide his fate."

"You know as well as I that he had the shanglo in his pocket, justice would not have been served. He had his kris Romani, a trial of Gypsy elders. The Romani served him his fate."

"Yes, Papa, you are right."

"Now what is for dinner today?"

"I have prepared a mas pie for you." I pulled it from the grate over the fire and removed it from the makeshift bov. The edges were browned perfectly. I served him in a bowl with a roj and a lovina I had on ice waiting for him."

"You spoil me."

"Yes, Papa, I do." I giggled. I saw my father slip Beau some of his meat pie. This made my heart happy.

"I went to see that fellow you are so found of today, Marcello. I asked him to help with the barn. He has agreed. So, I will get to know him as you have wished. By the way, I thought I heard a pup barking at his home."

"Maybe he has a rikono, Papa; I do not think that is a crime." I hoped I was flip enough that he did not suspect me, although I knew better. Possibly this was an opportunity for him to see what a fine man Marcello is. I could hope anyway.

I prepared my wares for the market. It would be an early morning and I had to walk far with my satchel of goods, and watch out for little Beau as well. I bid my father "Goodnight", and retired to bed. Beau curled up in his small bed and promptly fell asleep; I loved hearing his puppy snuffles as he slept. Sov over took me as well.

Chapter Thirteen

I awoke before daybreak and my father was up as well. He accompanied me into towne, parting ways on the outskirts. "Thank you for your help, Papa." I kissed him and continued to the market.

I set up shop and stepped back to evaluate my display. I bumped into someone and nearly fell. I felt strong arms catch me and steady me on my feet. I turned expecting to see Marcello, or Papa. To my surprise, I saw a very handsome young man around my age. He had long black hair and was wearing a mortsi hat, his skorni leather boots came to his knees, and he had a sash tied around his mashakar with a loose pirate shirt. He was definitely

Romani. His eyes were breathtaking, and I felt as if I had gotten lost in them. I pulled myself back to the present moment.

"Thank you for catching me, I am sorry I did not look before I tripped you." Beau began pulling at the young man's boot laces and growling. "I see my pup approves of your choice in footwear."

This made him laugh, and his voice had a rich, deep timbre to it.

"It was my pleasure. I am Manfri, and who might I have the pleasure of saving?"

"Oh, I beg your pardon, I am Crystobella. I did not mean to be rude."

He extended his hand and I took it.

"He tried to pull his hand back and I did not let go. He pulled again. "May I have my vast back?"

"Oh, I am so sorry, I am flustered after the near fall, please forgive me, again." I said, "Your name is interesting, what is its meaning?"

"It means man of peace."

"That is wonderful; well I shall dub you my Prince of Peace. Thank you again for saving me. I would like to give you a gift for your help."

He followed me to my stall. I handed him a citrine crystal and told him, "It will bring you happiness if you wear it near your heart."

"Thank you, Crystobella, I shall treasure it." He leaned to hug her and she allowed it. "I must be off now, my familia and I perform at the weekend faire and then again during the cirque. We are practicing today. We are the flying Gambians. You should catch our act."

I laughed at the pun. "I see; you must be a trapeze artist then."

"You are not only beautiful; you are smart as well." He tipped his hat and strode off.

I was embarrassed and a bit out of kintala. How could I have such strong feelings for this stranger when I had so much love for Marcello? I may wish to explore this friendship a bit. I would have the opportunity to do so in the next month, starting with this weekend's faire.

The day was long and I sold out of most of my tinctures and herbs. All of my bujos sold as well. I did not have much to pack up. I decided to carry Beau home. I bumped into my father and Marcello at the juncture home. "Hello, ryes."

"Hello, Faire Lady," said Marcello.

"Hello, Baby Bear," said Papa.

I inquired of their work. "How was your day, Fine Sirs?"

Marcello told me, "It was long and grueling, but I enjoyed spending time with your father."

Claude agreed. "Yes, we had an amicable day."

"I am glad to hear that," I intoned. Shall we walk together until the split?"

We began the journey home.

Marcello said, "Crystobella, I saw you with a fine young gentleman today in the market. Are you now betrothed?"

I thought, *he saw that?* "Oh, no, not at all. I fell back and he caught me. I was so clumsy and I am grateful to him for helping me stay on my feet."

"Ah, Baby Bear, perhaps he could be a worthy suitor, you will see him again, yes?"

"Papa, please!" I chastised him. "Yes, I shall see him again, though. He and his family are performing this weekend at the faire and during the cirque. They are trapeze artists. The flying Gambians."

"Impressive," said her father.

Marcello said, "Well I shall have to attend their show and see what all the fuss is about."

It was time for them to part ways. The pup was asleep in her arms, so she curtseyed to Marcello, "Good day."

"Good day to you, miss, and to you, Claude."

After Marcello took his leave Claude inquired, "Crystobella, do tell about your encounter with the schav today."

"Papa, there is really nothing to tell, I tripped and he caught me and righted me before I went to the ground."

"Angel, your eyes twinkle when you speak of him, now, tell your papa the tachiben."

"Ah, Papa, it is just an infatuation. I did think him handsome, but that is all, he is a stranger that helped me, that is all there is to tell."

"Ah, Baby Bear, we shall see, we shall see." He winked at her and then gave the pup a pat on the head.

We continued in silence until we reached camp.

"Papa! Do you see the horses? Where are the groi? Papa, they are gone!"

"Be calm my child, let us take a look around the kumpania."

I went directly to where they are staked and saw that the ropes had been severed. "Papa, the ropes have been severed; this looks like someone did this intentionally! Who would want to harm my beautiful horses?" My mind went immediately to the Mule. I will not give his name power, yet, it must be his doing. "Papa, it is the shimulo, I know it, I feel his presence, and he is a mulani with mal-intent."

"Crystobella, calm yourself dear child, the ropes look as if they may have broken, the horses must have been spooked and broke free, we will find them my dear. Let's begin the search in the waver."

"This may be so, Papa, yet, it is still the work of the mule, he is a mulani mal." We shall call in a mule-vi to speak with this mulani."

"Angel, you are able to converse with spirits, why must we call someone in?"

"Papa, he does not wish to converse with me, otherwise he would have done so, he wishes mal-intent on us ---"

He interrupted her, "Baby Bear, let us search and worry about the cause later."

We began by combing the woods, while I called out to them using a soft whistling sound. Madeleine came first; she trotted up to me and let out a soft snort. She nuzzled me. "Oh, my sweet mare, I am happy to find you, now lead us to Ganache." She turned and led me to a grove where there were some downed trees; Ganache was caught up by his loose rope on the branches. I ran to him calling, "Papa, help us, Ganache is stuck."

I inspected the horse and found he had a deep gash on his foreleg. "Father, he will need care, the gash is to the kokalo. It is a good thing I am able to help him heal with my medicines and drarnego, but I will need you to stitch him up, please."

"Baby Bear, let me help you untangle him and we will get them home so you can cleanse his wound and bed them down. Tomorrow I will purchase new rope for them, so they will be secure."

We led them back to camp. I set up my station near the fire so the needle could be sterilized in the yog, then I cleaned it with one of my concoctions. I threaded it with sinew and handed it to my father. "Mend him, Papa."

Luckily, he had not been into the bottle yet and his hand was steady. He stitched the wound up expertly; he'd had much practice as his habit of carousing got him into many a tavern brawl, and she refused to do it. When he finished, he said, "He is as good as new now, my angel."

"Thank you, Papa." I began applying a salve, and then covering it with honey. I used an old diklo to wrap as a bandage and keep the gash clean. Since ancient times honey has been used as an ointment that helps wounds to heal and prevents or draws out infection; I will reapply it to the wound daily. I will soak the hoof in one-part chote and three-parts water twice daily for pain relief.

I gave him a few drops of my antibiotic tincture in his grain. My magic tincture had garlic, honey, ginger, echinacea, goldenseal, clove, and oregano. I put molasses over it to hide the taste of the garlic and clove when Ganache snorted and refused to eat it. "Here you go my friend, some but-guli for your trauma." He began to eat his grain greedily after the addition of the molasses. I offered them each a drink from a bucket of pani nevi and after they drank, I gave them clean straw and returned to the fire where my father had begun to pi a bit of his rye whiskey that he had made in his kazan. It was going to be a long night.

"Papa, are you hungry?"

"Yes, Baby Bear, what is for supper?"

"I am tired after this long day, so will some bread, cheese, and fruit suffice?"

"Yes." He took a long swig from his bottle.

I fetched his food and sat down beside him with a plate for myself and glass of well-deserved wine. "Bon appétit."

"Sastimos." He replied. We ate for a few moments in silence. "I see that Marcello is khushti. I feel he is a man of his word and he has talent in woodworking."

"Oh, Papa! So, you like him?"

"I see that he is a rye. Yet, I would not welcome your tumnimos to him."

"But, Papa . . ."

"You have a thoximos to carry on the Gypsy name! We shall speak of this no more." He stood and said, "I shall see you later, don't wait up."

"Whiskey was a bad spirit, a mamioro to the body, mind, and soul." I said out loud, my father was gone and no one was there to hear me, except for my faithful new companion Beauregard. I scooped him up and lit a cigarette. I inhaled deeply, feeling the comfort of the tato smoke coursing through my lungs, I held it a moment and blew smoke rings into the air and watched as they floated away. Soon it was time for bed; I had much work to do to restock my wares for the weekend. I checked the horses and took Beau into the vurdon. I was in a dream world soon after.

In my dream the young man I had met that day, Manfri, he came to my stall and swept me into his arms and we travelled through the galaxy, he sat me upon a chakano. He joined me and we began to kiss. I was taken by his charm and wanted to be his butji. He placed a dickler around my neck and with a poof vanished into the darkness. I awoke with a start. How odd that dream was. I looked on the floor and saw a dickler lying there, one that I did not own. I picked it up and laid it beneath the pillow.

Chapter Fourteen

I looked over at my father's bunk; he was not home yet. Back to his philandering ways I thought with disgust. The rest of my night was spent in fitful unrest and I arose before the kham. Papa was still absent. I checked on the horses, they were resting comfortably. It was still too early to feed them, if they did not stick to a schedule, they could colic and she already had one down. It is a good thing they will not need to travel for a month, now. I must assemble my supplies and set to work.

It was afternoon when I finished the bujos. I got up to stretch and decided to change Ganache's bandage. He was a bit stiff, but otherwise it was already beginning to heal. I had to make herbal bundles and infuse them with dook. When that was finished, I decided to go into town and pick up some vegetables at the market to make some soup. I took the dickler from beneath my pillow and put it around my neck, it smelled manly. I set off for the market with Beau following behind, he was already growing bigger and he would bound around in circles as I walked, making me laugh.

When I reached the market, I picked him up and put him in the basket I had on my arm. While I was feeling the tomatoes for firmness, I bumped up against someone, I said, "Excuse me . . ." and turned to see Manfri! "Oh, we meet again."

"Yes, we do, and what a pleasure it is to see you once more."

I stuck out my vast to shake his and he saw my neck scarf. "Your dickler looks exactly like one I own, although it was missing this morning when I went to put it on."

"Are you accusing me of the choribe of your dickler?"

"Well, not exactly, but are you guilty? It appears that you are."

"However, would I have gotten your dickler? I have no idea where you stay."

He hadn't thought about that, "This is very tacho. Yet, it is in your possession . . ."

I said, "Shall we go to the café' and discuss this predicament? We will get to the tachiben of this matter; there must be a logical explanation."

We chose a table and he went to get us a pot of chao. When he returned he saw Beau in her lap. "I see you have you protector with you." Beau yipped at him and wagged his tail.

"I must confess something to you . . ."

"Ah, you wanted me sitting for the confession; you are a chor after all." He smiled and his eyes twinkled.

"Ah, you jest." I smiled back at him. I handed him the scarf and asked him, "Please, smell it."

He looked hesitant, but did as I asked of him. "Is this your scent?"

"No, I am not into putting perfumes on my skin."

"Most people that wear perfume are wealthy, as it is expensive for us commoners to do so."

He agreed, "Go on."

"You may keep your dickler, by the way. It was left in my room last night; I found it on the floor when I got out of bed. Did you visit me in the night?"

"My darling chavi, I most certainly did not!"

"I did not think so, now comes the confession: I am being haunted by a mulani, a mule, a very mal gajo. It smells of him!"

"And you believe he took my dickler and left it on your floor?"

"Yes, I had a streyino dream about you and I last night, we were flying in the galaxy and you set me upon a star. Then you kissed me and put your dickler around my neck, and then . . . well, and then you vanished into the darkness."

"This is quite a paramishus you tell. I must share a confession of my own now: "I am . . . how you say? I do not like women in a romantic fashion. I prefer homosexual eroticism."

I stuttered, "I, oh, I . . ."

"It is okay, most people are shocked to learn of this at first."

"I, no, I am not shocked, I am a bit relieved."

He raised an eyebrow at her. "You do not covet me then?" He laughed.

"No, nai, I do!" I blushed. I mean I would, but I am betrothed to a man, a gajo, and even though I thought I could fancy you . . . I am relieved that you are not available."

"I see." He looked at her with his perfect eyes and said, "I am sure your father does not approve of such a tumnimos."

"He does not. He wishes me to marry a Gypsy, and carry on the nav-romao."

"I have a proposition for you then."

"But you just told me you are into homosex ---"

He placed his hand over mine to stop my chattering. "Not that kind of proposition. One in which we both shall benefit from our betrothal. We announce that we are to be married, and we can even allow our families to throw an abiav, a wedding feast in our honor. That way I can secretly enjoy my erotic activities and you may enjoy yours, and no one will be the wiser. Our familia shall not bother us to continue on with the arranged marriage custom. It is a winning situation for all involved."

"Manfri. You are brilliant!"

I leaned across the table and kissed him. He looked stunned and asked me, "Did you already forget my preference?" Then he laughed a laugh with a deep timbre.

"No, I most certainly did not, yet, I feel we will be the best of friends, and we shall have to keep up appearances!"

"I did not think of that! I guess I shall have to get used to your affection."

At that moment Marcello walked up and asked in a gruff tone, "So keres, mi amor?" He looked directly at me and then at the young man.

We said in unison, "We can explain!"

"Please do!"

"Have a seat, my love." He did as I asked and Manfri went to get him a kafa. I began the explanation, "Manfri just gave us a solution to our problem with Papa, He is a homosexual, and his family is pushing him to marry a Gypsy girl, just as Papa is pushing me to marry a Gypsy boy. They have noticed that we are attracted to one another, yet, they do not know it is just as friends, as kindred souls! If we are betrothed, then they will not look into our activities too closely, that gives you and I **Slobuzenja** and Manfri and . . ."

He had just walked up and said, "Giovanni, he is my one true love."

Marcello looked at him with shock, yet, he smiled and turned back to his love. "Mi amor, this is good news."

"Yes, just last night, Papa was telling me he liked you, but would not tolerate us being together. So, this is very good news."

We lifted our cups and made a toast. "To the twist of fate that has bound us together, and allowed us each to follow our heart's desire!"

We chatted for a few more minutes and then we parted ways. Marcello had to return to the construction site, I needed to get my vegetables, and I presumed Manfri was headed to tell Giovanni his good news. Oh, how I love fate, at least when it works in my favor.

Chapter Fifteen

I was stirring the soup when my father came back, he was in a foul mood, his hangovers from the whiskey were worse than his drunkenness. "What is for supper?"

"Papa, I have made zumi, it will be ready in a few moments. I have made a salad to start, I handed him a plate, and he knocked it to the ground. "I will not eat rabbit food girl!"

I began to cry and through my tears told him, "You should appreciate me while you have me, for soon I shall be married and live with my betrothed. I will no longer be yours to shav around!"

He stood up and raised his hand to her, "If you think you will marry that gajo, you will think again!" He swung at her and she blocked him with a log she had picked up to defend herself.

"That will be the last time you ever raise a hand to me, Papa."

"He hung his head into his hands and began to weep: "I am so sorry, my angel, my Baby Bear. I miss your mother so much and sometimes it angers me that you look so much like her . . .""

"That is no excuse; I shall not join your pity party, Papa." I turned back to my pot of zumi. I had a loaf of moro warming in my makeshift oven on top of the grate. I tore a piece off for my father and handed him his soup, "xa," I told him. "If you throw this one to the ground you will never receive another meal from me."

He looked up and pleaded with her. "Forgive me, Baby Bear. I am sorry, I love you, and I will love you for eternity."

I felt sorry for the mess I called my dat; I went to him and embraced his shoulders. "I love you Papa, yet, I shall not tolerate this behavior again. I will leave with my husband and you shan't ever see me again, do you understand this?" I patted his back and said, "You are forgiven."

We both ate in silence; Beau was even quiet, curled up by the fireside on a rug.

He finally said, "Who is the lucky man, if not Marcello?"

"It is the chava, the Gypsy boy, Manfri, one of the flying Gambians!"

Her father looked up surprised at her revelation, at once the look of surprise was replaced with joy! "I am so happy, Angel! We must have a party! A pliashka!"

"Manfri will come here with his familia after the faire this weekend. He will ask you for my hand and then you and his parents can work out the details of the abiav and chiez."

"Perfect!" exclaimed Claude.

"Now Papa, if you do not mind, I have a date with my love."

"Yes, Baby Bear, go to him."

By saying my love, I was telling no lie, even though it was a bit deceitful, it was not a lie. I headed toward the towne, but at the fork darted off into the wood, winding my way to Marcello. I tapped on his door and he flung it open picking me up and whisking me inside. He flung me onto the bed. There was a fire in the fireplace beside the bed and he had champagne chilled on the table with two glasses and some lolo mura.
"How romantic, darling!" I exclaimed. "I am so in love with you."

"He replied "And I with you, mi amor." *He pounced on her and did not even bother to remove her skirts, he reached beneath them and pulled her petticoats down and entered her mish, while she tore at his shirt and the kochos flew off, hitting the dila, where Beau chased them.* Yet, no one noticed as we were engulfed in passion.

I bit at his nipples and then at his neck as he pulled my breast from my blouse and began to suckle it as he thrust into me. It was hard and fast, moments later we both lay spent on the bed. He handed me champagne and the puppy cried to join us.

I chastised Beau, "Now, now, my furry boy, this is our time. You lie by the fire and be content. Miro, my little one."

I snuggled closer to Marce' telling him, "In your arms is where I wish to spend eternity." He bent over me and kissed me once more. I pulled him to me and he entered me again. Soon after we fell asleep in one another's arms.

I awoke at day break, "Oh, no I must go now! Papa will have my hide!"

"Amor, he will think you were with your betrothed, do not worry." He kissed her and helped her gather her things.

"I must make my way to the market today!"

"I shall see you later, mi amor."

I wound my way through the kahst and came out at the fork in the road where I bumped into my betrothed.

"Fate is a fanciful thing!" I squealed. What perfect timing. "Shall you accompany me to my vurdon?"

"I shall, my lady." We hooked arms and went toward the kumpania. I asked him "What shenanigans were you up to last night?"

"The best kind," he replied. And we both giggled.

When we arrived, Claude was up and getting ready for work. I hoped he still had a job after his absence yesterday. "Papa, there is someone I would like you to meet."

Claude stepped over to the pair and stuck out his hand. "I am pleased to meet you, young man."

Manfri took his hand and replied, "I am equally as pleased, sir. I am Manfri." He added, "I am sorry to have your daughter home at such a late, or albeit early hour. We fell asleep staring at the satarmas."

"It is okay zhamutro, I once had tenimos as well. Thank you for returning her safely."

"I shall take my leave now, sir, my Angel. I have an appointment with the ferari to make our angustris."

We both looked at Manfri aghast. "Young man . . ." began Claude.

"I jest. I have an appointment with the gabori. Such a fine mort, mira, fine mort, deserves a ring befitting a queen." He took her hand and kissed it, declaring "You are now my queen of the Gypsies!"

I giggled and said, "Later miri flying king." He tipped his hat and strode away.

Papa looked at me and said, "It is good to see you so baxtalo. It reminds me of when I met your mother . . ." A look of sadness crossed his face, but he recovered well. "I am happy for you, Baby Bear."

"Papa, I must get to the weekend faire. I will see you this evening." I kissed him on the cheek, gathered my things and Beau, and we set off to towne.

Claude wondered why her betrothed did not wait for her. But remembered he had an appointment, and besides his Crystobella was a strong, independent mort.

As I walked to the towne I felt the mal presence following me. I began to incant a prayer to ward it off. That mule needs to go. I used the circle of light prayer: *"The light of God surrounds us. The love of God enfolds us. The power of God protects us. The presence of God watches over us. Wherever we are, God is. All is well."*

I felt a bit better, yet, knew that the prayer did not dissuade it. When I arrived at the faire grounds, I set up the ofisa and called in the dook. I had several clients that day and sold many bujos, of this I was glad. After all, we had a wedding feast to plan. Although, I am worth a daro paid by the familia of the groom, we must also afford the wedding as the father of the bride is normally responsible for that.

I had a few customers come for salve and tinctures, and one more person to read for. A young woman of wealth sat down on my chair, she looked familiar. "Do I know you?"

"No, we have never met. I am from Versailles."

I gasped. "I am sorry, I just had a bug bite my leg," I lied.

"I am here because my sister, Adrienne, saw you when you were in Versailles. She has had wonderful luck since then. Her cad of a husband ran off with one of his prostitutes, and she was able to annul the marriage, thus saving her fortune and also find a new love; one that adores her."

I thought, well, that is good nevipe. They still think the devil has run off back in Versailles. I replied, "Well, I am not in the business of getting rid of husbands, but I can read for you and see what your energy tells me. You may also purchase a bujo, medicine bag, crystal, or charm to assist your luck. Shall we see what the universe holds for you?"

The woman nodded and said, "Well, I do not have a husband to be rid of. I am seeking to find one that I shall cherish, as my sister has."

"Let us begin." I lit a candle and said a prayer; I asked the woman her name. "Your name please."

"Aloysia."

"Thank you. Aloysia, place your hands beside mine on the crystal ball so they are touching. Now do you give me permission to enter your energetic field?"

"Yes, of course."

"I see a man in your future, actually he is already around you, and you have not noticed him though, as he is not of your class."

Aloysia nodded. "Yes, yes, there is someone I love, but our parents, mine, and Adrienne's; they have forbidden me to marry him. He is a good man. I have given up hope of being with him, although I shall always love him."

"A message is coming in for you, "Your priorities are not aligned with your greater good. You must listen to and follow the guidance of your heart. They tell me that you can be with him, yet, you will lose your inheritance if that is the case."

"That is true." A tear began to form and she dabbed at her eye with an intricately woven handkerchief.

"Where there is a will there is a way. Perhaps, do you have a friend, one that is not a romantic interest, but who is in the same situation?"

"Why, what are you thinking?"

"Hear me out. If you have someone close to you that you trust, ask him to be your betrothed, and then see the man you love. The charade shall end with your parent's deaths and you and your love can then be together and keep your inheritance. I see that you will have your sister's blessing once your parents pass on."

She thought about what Crystobella had said and then answered her. "I do have a dear, dear friend. He is my closest confidant. My parent's wish me to marry him, but he is also in love with another. She is a servant girl."

"Then your problem is solved."

She stood and gave Crystobella a hug over the table. Sitting back down she said, "YOU are a genius, yet a bit of a deceitful genius. It will work, though, I know it will."

"I am normally not a deceitful person, yet, where love is concerned, I feel when people try to bend it to their will and control who loves whom, it is going against the laws of nature and against God. I am offering you a short-term solution for long-term happiness." She asked for two protection charms and then said "No, make that four; I shall give one to each of our love members."

I stood, and handed her a small silk satchel with the bujos. And there were a few rhodochrosite crystals inside for each one of them. "Keeping this crystal near your heart will keep your love safe. It will protect your heart."

Aloysia kissed her on the cheek and dropped a demi-louis and ten ècus in her palm. "I cannot take this, you have over paid me."

"You can, and you will. My sister sent the demi-louis for you, as you have done her a great service." At that moment a wind blew into the ofisa and the white candle blew out. It startled both women. Aloysia continued, I must return to Hôtel Matignôn, I am there for an aristocratic event. I slipped away as this was the real reason for my journey here; the ball is just a cover. Good day, my dear." She slipped out of the ofisa and was gone.

The candle blowing out was the mule, I knew it, but he would not win. I gathered my things and set out for home, but became distracted when I saw the tserha the Gambians were in. I pulled back the flap and peered within. I saw my betrothed flying through the air on the great trapeze, another man was hanging upside down and caught him by his wrists and they 'flew' together and then the man let him go; Manfri did a triple flip, turning and catching his trapeze once again. Beau jumped from my arms and rain into the tserha. I had no choice but to follow.

Chapter Sixteen

I pushed the flap of the tent aside and ran in after him, I nearly had him, but he slipped under the bleachers and made his way to the center of the ring . . . I stood at the edge not knowing what to do. The audience loved Beau and they began to cheer and clap. I looked up and saw Manfri laughing, he flipped through the air, and landed in the net, after bouncing a few times, he expertly caught the edge and flipped to the ground taking a bow and scooping up the pup.

He pointed his arm towards me, and announced in his booming voice: "Crystobella, please come here."

I walked into the ring, feeling quite embarrassed. He then took my arm and gave me a kiss on the cheek. "I would like you all to meet my betrothed, the magnificent Crystobella!" I took a bow and made a curtsey. He handed me Beau, "And that would be our first child, he is a bit hairy, but we love him." The crowd roared at his humor. He looked up to his father and mother who were still on the platform and said, "I had wanted to break the news to you in a less surprising way, but I would love for you to meet my future bride."

The Gambians jumped into the air doing an intricate air dance and landed in the net, before flipping to the ground and joining their son. They told the crowd, "We had no idea you had such a lovely prospect for a wife. We love the surprise, but hope you will have better looking and less hairy children in the near future." The audience roared once more. They took turns hugging Crystobella and thanked everyone for being a part of their grand surprise. "We will return shortly for our next act."

Manfri escorted me to the changing area backstage. He said, "What a surprise, love," as his parents were within hearing.

"I know, my dear. I just missed you and hoped to get a glimpse before I went home tonight, but Beauregard had other plans, I guess."

He kissed me on the mouth to my surprise and said, "I will see you later, my dear. And you too, little Beau." He patted the dog on the head.

His parents called to him, "We must be ready to go on in three minutes son."

He nodded.

I said, "Nice to have met you, we must meet again in a more formal setting."

They assured me we would, "Good evening, dear."

I made my way to the exit and began the journey home. I had never been part of a cirque performance before and I found it quite thrilling. Maybe I would have to join the act after the wedding. I giggled at the thought. Me on the trapeze! Beauregard might as well be part of the act too. I pictured him flying through the air, and that brought me to full laughter.

My father was at the camp when I arrived. He said, "I have lost my job, Bella."

"Oh, Papa,"

"I cannot seem to keep a job for long."

"Papa, it is the drink, if you limit it, you will keep a job. Do not worry, I had a good day at the faire." I handed him a few livre.

He hugged me.

"Papa, please don't waste it on drinking and women."

"I will not, my Baby Bear."

But I knew better. He headed over to the shaving station and dabbed on some oil. I knew exactly where he was going. Thankfully, I kept my other earnings secreted away from him, or we would all starve.

After he left for the night, I decided to go to Marcello's. First, I had to take care of my horses. I re-bandaged Ganache's wound and made sure they had food and water. I checked their ropes and they were strong. I felt confident in leaving for the evening.

I went directly to Marcello's via the path way. My father would not be spying on me now, especially with galbi in his potchee. My beloved answered the door and hugged me, ushering me in from the cold evening air. It was only September, yet, it felt like November tonight. There was a storm brewing and the wind had whipped my hair around my face. Marcello commented, "You have a wild look about you tonight, mi amor."

"It is the wind, my love, and I am pahome! I am chilled to my kokalos.

He led me to the fireside. He stood facing me and embraced me, planting a kiss on my forehead. We stood like that for a while.

I finally broke the embrace. "My love, I am so happy to be able to spend my nights with you. I wish that it would be as your wife, but alas, we must continue with our charade. It is our safety blanket. I am grateful for our time together."

He said, "Wait here, mi amor, I shall return in a moment." I enjoyed the warmth of the yog as I waited. He came back with a box; it had a ribbon around it. He presented it to me. "For you, an early wedding present," he teased her.

I untied the ribbon and opened it to reveal a beautifully made cedar box. It was intricately carved on the outside with a forest scene, and adre, it was lined with velvet. A tear escaped my eye and I exclaimed, "I love it! It is exquisite!"

"I must show you the best part. He opened the box again and pushed on the side panel, the false bottom popped up and there was a place for me to keep my drawings and other secret treasures. Inside the hidden compartment sat a small box; I opened it and saw the most beautiful ring I had ever laid eyes upon. It was a crown setting and high quality rose gold. There was an emerald in the center and many small diamonds surrounding the setting. "When you are to wed Manfri, please use this ring. This was my mother's ring and her mothers before her. I want mi amor de mi Vida to wear it proudly. No one need know it was not from Manfri."

"I am honored, my love. It is a beautiful sumadji." I put it on.

He said, "Please take it off." When he saw the look of shock on her face, he added, "Just so I may place it properly on your hand."

I removed it and handed it to him. He held it near my finger as he supported my hand and recited his vow. "With this ring, a symbol of my love, a circle, representing eternity without end, I take you as my wife, to have and to hold from this day forth. I will protect you and keep you, in sickness and in health, forsaking all others. I love you with all of my heart and all of my soul." He placed the ring on my finger."

I produced the demi-louis. "With this symbol of my love, a circle, representing eternity, I take thee as my husband. To have and to hold from this day forth, in sickness and in health; forsaking all others. I shall love you even with my dying breath and will meet you in eternity." I placed it in his left palm and closed his fingers over it. "It is the most valuable thing I own, besides my Beau and the horses. I want you to keep it close to your heart my love."

He told me he would make a small hole in it and put it on a chain so it would always lie near his heart. He kissed me with a fierceness that set me on fire. I pulled him to the floor and we consummated the marriage right then and there, in front of the fire and Beau.

Later I had to tell him, "I must go now my love, it will be another long day at the faire tomorrow and Manfri is bringing his famailia to meet my father after their show ends. It is our plochka, an engagement feast where the father and sastro work out the details of the daro; I hope I fetch a good price!"

I kissed him good night and went out the door with Beau on my heels. On my way home I felt chilled again. My bones ached and I felt a bit of naswalemos. I still felt the presence nearby. Beau whimpered and I picked him up. I ran to get out of the waver. Once I reached the edge, I slowed my pace. I was happy to come home to the camp. It was calm and the horses were resting peacefully. I went into the wagon and my father was sitting at his desk. "Papa, what a surprise. I had thought you were out for the night."

"I went to see an old friend and we had a round of lovina, but I am home now, Baby Bear."

He glanced at her hand and saw the ring. "What is on your finger?"

"Oh, no, I forgot to give the wedding ring back to Manfri, he asked me to try it on so he could present it tomorrow when he brings his parents to meet you!"

"I am sure he will understand when you slip it into his pocket so no one notices you saw it before the proposal, angel."

"You are right, Papa." I held it out to him. "Isn't it lovely?"

"He inspected it and marveled at the beauty. "This must have been expensive; the Gambians must be loaded from their cirque act."

"He told me it has been in the family for generations, a sumadji, he took it to the jeweler to be repaired and polished. I think it is perfect."

"It is my darling. I brought home a chicken and cooked it on the spit if you'd like to have some."

"Thank you, Papa, but my stomach is a bit upset. I am not feeling well."

"Then you should rest, my Baby Bear, you have to be well for your client's tomorrow."

I turned and went to my bed. My father infuriated me at times. All he seemed to care about was the clients and the money. Yes, he said he loved her, but he had an odd way of showing it. I fell asleep and dreamt of my one tacho love, Marcello. We were happy and living together in his cottage, my beloved horses were in the field, and Beauregard was on the stoop. When morning came, I did not want to get up. I wished to live in my dream world forever. I did get up though; I had to tend to my clients.

Chapter Seventeen

I tried to see Manfri before the day began, but he was not at the cirque tserha. I realized I did not know where he actually lived, and he was supposed to be my betrothed! I had a few less clients than yesterday, but my sales of herbs and tinctures were good and I already sold all of the bujos. Beau was under the table; he was curled up and sleeping. I was still feeling queasy. I put up a small sign stating I would return and stepped away to get some ginger chao.

After the day ended, I slipped over to the Gambian tent. I lifted the flap near the dressing room and made the noise "PSSST." Thankfully Manfri heard me and he came over. I whispered in his ear, "I have had a ceremony with Marcello, he gave me his grandmother's ring, I told my father it was your grandmother's and I forgot to give it back after you had me try it on."

"I was having a ring made, it is just a band of gold, not expensive, but nice."

"Have the jeweler make it for you. I will slip this into your pocket when you arrive with your familia tonight. And by the way, you also gave me a beautifully carved box, and it was commissioned from Marcello if anyone asks." I gave him a peck on the cheek and said, "See you later." Beau stayed by his feet. I whistled and he reluctantly came to me.

"It seems he likes me more than he likes you, well at least someone does." He laughed his infectious laugh. And I could hear it even when I was a half block away.

I went home and made a delicious supper with the left over kanny. I had purchased some corn meal and made xaritsa in the little homemade bov. I added potatoes with herbs and garden peas. I found a bottle of our best wine, well, best may not describe it accurately, but it will do, I thought. I decided to add a few herbs to the wine, a bit of lavender will give it a nice flavor.

My father was late as usual, and he strolled in a bit tipsy. "Papa, you were to be on your best behavior tonight. The familia of Manfri are going to be here any minute!"

"I will be fine, Baby Bear," He said and then hiccupped!

What shall I do? I made a pot of kafa on the fire and made my father drink two cups. It seemed to sober him up a bit. "Now, go get ready, Papa, please!"

He came back just as the familia Gambian arrived. Introductions were made and everyone sat around a makeshift dining table. I served them the dinner I had prepared. Mrs. Gambian commented, "You are a good cook, my dear, and these herbs are exquisite, you must share your recipe."

"Certainly, Mrs. Gambian."

"Please, call me Claire."

"Okay," I said meekly.

"You may call Mr. Gambian grouchy," she teased. "But seriously you may call him Antonio."

"You have a French name and He has an Italian name. Would you mind telling me what brought the two of you together. I am a romantic at heart and would love to hear the story." I knew from Manfri that his mother was from a wealthy family and left her moneyed manush to join the cirque, which is where she met Antonio.

Claire began. "I had dreamed of being a performer in the cirque since I was a small girl. I thought perhaps I would be in a sparkling outfit riding on the grand white horses with plumes in their manes, but when the cirque came to town, they needed a trapeze artist. I decided to try out. Well of course, I was not trained and fell to the net every time I tried to perform a feat. But I met Tony, and I was smitten. He liked me too, so I told him I would run away with him if he would train me to fly on the trapeze. The rest is history." She smiled at her husband.

"What about your parents?" Claude asked.

"Oh, well, I told them I was going to join the cirque, they laughed and thought I was joking. I told them I was serious. They said 'if you do so you are disowned, there will be no inheritance, and they no longer had a daughter.' That was nearly thirty years ago. I would not have changed my life for the world."

Claude continued, "The ring must have come from Antonio's side of the familia."

"Wha . . ." began Claire, and Manfri quickly cut in.

"Yes, mama, father's grandmother's ring, it has been passed down from generation to generation. I am going to present it tonight after I ask for Crystobella's hand in marriage. You no longer need to keep it a secret."

She looked a bit confused but recovered well. "Ah, yes my son, I did not want to spill the bobas." She did not know what her son was up to, but she would go along with it for now and find out later just exactly what was going on.

He said, "Before we have dessert and drinks, Claude, I would like to address you, sir. "May I have the vast of your pakvora Daughter in marriage?"

Claude replied, "You have my blessing, zhamutro. You have made me baxtalo."

He knelt before Crystobella. "Will you accept this angustri and become my bori?"

"Yes! Yes! I will!" I grabbed him and planted a kiss on his lips that he would never forget!

He slipped the ring on my finger and exclaimed, "Then we shall have a celebration! Break out the vino!"

I announced, "I have made ambrols de glace' for dessert." I served the pears while my betrothed served the wine."

My father and Antonio had their seros together for a long while, most likely discussing the darro.

Everyone had a most enjoyable evening and it was time to bid our guests good night. The adults looked at the young couple in expectation. Manfri grabbed his bride to be and kissed her with a passion he did not feel. The adults looked appeased. The Gambian family went on their way.

"I am happy that part is over!"

"When are you two planning on holding the ceremony?"

"Well, Papa, I should think right after the month-long cirque ends. It will begin to get cold as it will be the middle of October. After all, we do not want to wait too long."

"Will you be leaving me, Baby Bear?"

"No, Papa. Only when the cirque is traveling of course. Manfri and I have decided to get our own vurdon and park it here. We will share the kumpania with you and the Natsia. You will not lose me, have no fear, Papa, I shall still care for you."

"It is Gypsy custom for you to join his familia."

"Yes, Papa, I know how you love to stay with tradition. Yet, neither he nor I wish to adhere to Gypsy custom, Papa. We will start our own traditions. You should be happy that at least we are carrying on the nav-ramano."

"Yes, child, you are right, I will count my blessings. I will also be on the lookout for a cheap vurdon we can fix up for the two of you; Antonio has agreed to share the cost as your darro."

"Thank you, Papa, but remember Ganache will not be healed for at least four more weeks to bring it here."

"I can ask Antonio to borrow a team if I find one suitable for the two of you, my angel . . . and my zhamutro."

Chapter Eighteen

I realized I could not slip away to see my love, Marce' tonight. I would find a way to see him tomorrow. He will be pleased I am officially wearing his ring. I was exhausted from the nights festivities and it was bed time, sov was about to overtake me. I trudged into the vurdon and Beau bounded up the stairs and jumped on my bed. I had not realized how much he had grown. He would need to learn his bed was on the floor, especially now with his size.

"Down! Down boy!" I pointed to his bed, he looked at me sideways as if he did not understand and lie on my bed. "Beau, down, to your bed, now!" This time he acquiesced and jumped to the floor slinking to his bed. He looked so dejected; I gave him a pat on the head and lie down myself.

My stomach was aching and felt swollen; I was also feeling queasy again. I may have to see the doctor as my remedies were not alleviating my distress. Maybe the mule was a mamioro after all. I will go to the physician if I am not feeling better in the morning.

I woke up in the night and vomited just outside the door, Beau began to whimper, and Papa shifted in his sleep. "Baby Bear, are you ailing?"

"It is okay, Papa, I am just feeling a bit of distress in my stomach. I fear it may be johai. The ghost vomit. I will chew on some ginger and lie back down.

"Aah, Baby Bear . . . that again? Okay, good night."

"I lay there looking at my wo-man-made galaxy. I wonder what it would be like to live there, among the stars. I finally fell back to sleep. I awoke feeling even worse the next day. I told my father, "I must go in to see the physician, Papa. Could you feed the horses please?"

"Of course, Baby Bear. If you can wait until I am done, I can go with you."

"No, Papa, I will be okay, please take care of the horses and Beau, please."
I looked at Beau who was at my feet looking up at me expectantly. "Besh, Beau, Besh! You must stay here today."

I had to keep stopping on the way to the Doctor's office from weakness. I finally arrived and knocked on the door; a nurse opened the door and saw how pale I was. "Come in dear, and have a seat. I will fetch the doc."

She returned with a distinguished looking gentleman, he helped me up. "Come with me into the examination room, please."

He helped me onto his table, "Now, what seems to be troubling you, young miss?

"I have been feeling queasy as of late, and my stomach is tender. My legs have been swelling a bit as well. I am an herbalist, but my tinctures are not working."

"If it is what I suspect it is, a tincture won't cure it; only giving birth will."

I looked stricken. "What?" I began to cry, "No, oh, no. Nai!"

The nurse tried to comfort me, "It will be okay, dear one. It is natural after all."

I explained between sobs. "You don't understand. I was raped in Versailles by a vile man. I am now betrothed, what will I tell my fiancé'?"

"Lay back now, my dear, so the doc can examine you."

I did as I was told. I flinched when I felt a cold metal object be inserted within my mish. He peered in with his headlamp, and then I felt him poking around. "Yes, just as I suspected, you are about three months along now dear."

I began to sob harder. He gave me something to calm my nerves. It made me feel streyino and very odd. The nurse helped me up. "We can only recommend you take ginger for your nausea and hope it will subside in your second trimester. Make sure you are getting good nutrition, and drink water and milk, dear."

"What do I owe you?"

The nurse looked at the doc and back at Crystobella. "No charge today, dear."

"Oh, but I insist, I have the money to pay. Please allow me to pay for your services."

"If you insist, one livre."

I knew they were being kind and paid them what they asked, even though it could not have been the normal fee. I must go to Manfri and Marcello, but who first? What a mess I was in. Manfri's parents will think the child is his, Marcello may be the father, but most likely it was that vile shimulo! I stopped by the cirque tserha first.

"Manfri, my love, are you here?"

He came to the door flap. "What is it, my darling bride to be?"

"I just came from the doctor and I am expecting our first child." She wanted to keep up appearances in case someone was eavesdropping.

He looked stunned, but said, "I am so happy; it will be the first child that is not hairy! Where is the hairy beast by the way?"

I laughed. "I love you so, I am glad you can have a sense of humor about this."

He whispered in my ear. "We may need to have the wedding before the cirque next week, to make sure you are not the talk of the towne."

"Okay, you can speak to your parents and I will speak with my Papa."

I kissed him on the cheek and told him, "I will see you later, dear."

Chapter Nineteen

I went straight to Marcello's next. He answered the door after three knocks. "I am sorry amor; I was in back working in my woodshop." He saw my tear streaked face. "What is troubling you?"

"Marce', I have just come from the doctor, I have been queasy as of late, I vomited last night. He examined me and I am with child!"

"This is a good thing, mi amor!"

"Well if it was your child, yes, it would be a good thing, but what if it is the spawn of the man who violated me?"

"I will love the child just the same."

"You are a great man, Marcello. I do not deserve such a prince as my husband."

"But you do. I love you with all my heart."

"You do realize that Manfri's parents are going to think this is his child. You will have to be the God-father and will not be able to acknowledge him in public."

"I know, mi amor, and I am okay with it. We will make this work and the child will know much love."

"Thank you, I love you into infinity." I kissed him and then ran to the door and vomited again.

He made a joke about my reaction to his kiss. "It is not you my love, it is the morning-sickness, or in my case, the all-the-time-sickness!"

"I must tell Papa; I am sorry to leave you so soon. He is watching Beau and We are moving the wedding up, so I am not talked about behind closed doors or worse become a marime, an outcast."

I kissed him again and left.

He called after me. "I am glad you did not have a bad reaction to my kiss that time, amor!" He waved at me, as I slipped into the woods.

I waved back and blew him a kiss. It was tough to travel so much in one day while feeling so poorly. I was happy to arrive home. Beau ran up to me and began to paw at my legs trying to get me to pick him up. "You are growing big, my friend, I cannot lift you now, besh!" She bent down and placed a kiss on his head. "Papa, Papa, are you here?"

He came out of the vurdon. "Yes, Baby Bear, what did the doctor say?"

"Oh, Papa, I am with child." I went and hugged him.

He patted my back to comfort me. "It will be okay. No one will suspect."

"I know Papa, Manfri and I decided to move the wedding up to next week, just before the cirque begins,"

"That will be fine. I also found a nice vurdon for you and your kirvi. Antonio is having it delivered tomorrow."

"Thank you, Papa, I must rest now." I thought to myself, I hope I feel better soon, this is agony. I would like to enjoy my wedding, even if it is a paramicha. I fell asleep and rested for quite some time. When I awoke, I decided to go and see Manfri and his mother. If we were to be married in the next week, we should do some planning. I stood up and felt a bit dizzy, but it soon passed. I did feel better in the evenings, and decided that is when I will have to be the most productive.

I found the Gambians in their tent practicing a new act for the upcoming cirque. "Hello, familia, sar san?"

Claire gave me a hug. Antonio yelled a greeting from the platform and Manfri came bounding down off of the net with a flourish. He came and embraced me, giving me a peck on the cheek.

"I would like to do a bit of wedding planning if you have a few moments, Claire."

"My darling bori, I shall have the abiav catered. We will hold it here in the tserha. The only thing I will need you to do is to invite your side of the familiyi. I believe you will also need a Rom Baro to perform the ceremony. You and Manfri must go to the church parish house and record your marriage."

"My sero is spinning! There is so much that goes into a wedding!"

"My dear, you only need to do those few things I asked of you and show up on Saturday. You may leave the party planning to me. I have looked forward to this day since the birth of Manfri. We are all baxtalo!"

"I have not thought of what dress to wear." I looked sad for a moment, but recovered. "I had hoped to wear my mother's, but according to Gypsy custom, it was burned after her passing."

"I still have mine, I was once a young girl, and about your size; shall we go see if it fits?" Claire informed the men that they would be going to the home for a bit and would return soon.

"Manfri, be ready to escort your bori to the parish house at the church to record your marriage when we return."

"Yes, Mother, I shall be ready." He blew a kiss in the general direction of the ladies.

"See you soon, my love," I replied, blowing him a kiss as well.

When we arrived at the house of the Gambians, Crystobella was pleased that it was understated and quaint. It was the second building on a Manor residence. It was a small stone A-frame with large arched window panes. Inside it was equipped with a small kitchen area and a large fireplace, cozy throws and sheranda adorned the sparse furnishings. A wrought iron chandelier hung in the center of the vaulted ceiling and there was a staircase to the right of the entrance that led upstairs to two loft bedrooms. Claire led the way up the stairs. "Be careful, dear, these are steep."

We arrived at the first bedroom; it had a bed and no door and it overlooked the downstairs. "This is Manfri's room, you can tell by the state it is in that a man occupies it," she laughed fondly. The next room had a door, Claire opened it, and we entered. "This is our room, and here in this trunk we shall find your treasure."

She opened the trunk and pulled out the most beautiful dress I had ever laid eyes upon. It was made of off-white velvet and had an open, square neck of the Tudor style. The sleeves were long and belled at the ends with intricate embroidery; there were embellishments around the neckline and breasts as well. The waist was small and the hips had an overskirt that had embellishments too. The skirt formed a slight train and the underskirt was made of white lace, embellished with crystals that shone like diamonds. "This is kind of you to allow me to wear this beautiful gown! I shall feel like a princess . . . a Gypsy princess!"

"Please try it on." She handed it to me. "It is the second sumadji you have received for your abiav. Where did the angustri come from? I am sure it is not Antonio's grandmother's ring."

I pretended not hear as I took the gown to the chaise lounge and gently laid it down. I removed my bohemian clothing and then carefully donned the dress. It fit me superbly.

I finally spoke about the ring. "I am sorry we deceived you Claire, but you know that I am not allowed to keep anything from those that have departed, as is our custom. Yet, my puri daj left me some things that Papa does not know about, I am not one to keep with tradition, nor was she. She was a rebel, and I love her."

Claire responded, "It is fine darling, I thought it was something like that. Now let's have a look at you." Claire exclaimed, "It was as if it was made for you! This marriage must have been written in the stars; it was meant to be!"

I smiled, even though I felt awful knowing the deception Manfri and I were perpetrating. I twirled around and then hugged my future mother -in-law.

I stepped back to ask Claire a question. "Did Manfri tell you the reason why we are to wed so quickly?"

Claire nodded. "He told us you are with child. We are pleased, even if it is not in the order most prefer. You see, Toni and I also were with child when we wed and it has only made us more in love. You have our blessings my dear bori." She kissed her on the cheek and said now let's get back so you and Manfri can get your papers in order."

"Thank you, Dya." Claire smiled at my use of the title and touched my face with her palm.

Manfri was in his dressing room when we returned and he and I set off for the church.

"Manfri, I feel distress at the thought of deceiving your parents. They think that this grandchild is yours and he will carry on the Gambian name."

"Do not fret dear Crystobella, this is their only chance at having a grandchild, they will show the baby much love, and they will not utter a word, even if they suspect it is not my child."

"I would feel better if we tell them about the rape and explain that you are standing by my side even in the face of this pregnancy."

"I shall do as you wish, yet, I do not feel it will matter to my parents."

"I know in my heart you are correct, yet, it would ease my fears if we explain this situation to them. When we get back, I would like your support in revealing the truth, as it is bad enough our marriage is a lie, two would only compound my guilt."

We knocked on the parish door; a plump woman dressed in a katrinsa answered the door. "May I help you?" She inquired.

"We are here to record our marriage."

"Please come in and wait here, I will fetch the parish priest." She scurried off and we waited in the vestibule. A few moments later she returned with the priest in tow, he was equally plump and jolly. "Here he is," she said unceremoniously.

I am Father Bovary. My housekeeper does not mean to be rude, she is just forgetful," He chuckled and then led them to his office. "This way, young ones."

We followed him into his much-cluttered office space. He shuffled through papers and drawers and finally produced a paper for us to fill in the blanks where information was needed. It required much information!

Manfri read it. "It says here we must list our witnesses. But they have not witnessed the wedding yet, as it is this Saturday."

"No worries, son, they can come in after the wedding ceremony and sign the document. I will wait to file it."

He wrote on the paper eloquently, Name of Groom, name of spouse, name of parent's, marriage date, occupation, birthplace of each of them, their birthdates, the residence of each of their father's and when he came to the witnesses, he looked at his bride to be. "Who shall our witnesses be, darling?"

"I will suggest Giovanni and Marcello."

He looked at her with shock, yet, said, "Perfect."

"They are our best friends. Who better to be our official witnesses?"

He nodded his agreement and wrote their names in the space provided. He handed the document to the priest. Here you are Father Bovary.

"Well, young ones, I will wait to sign this when you and your witnesses sign and then you will be legally registered as man and wife."

"Thank you, father. We will see you on Sunday to finish our paper work."

"That will be fine as long as you wait until after mass."

"It shall not be early," added Manfri, "After all, it is the morning after our wedding night!"

The priest winked at him. "Thank you again father, see you Sunday, late afternoon."

He escorted me, his bori, out of the parish house. We continued to walk arm and arm to keep up appearances. "I sometimes wish our wedding were real," I confessed.

"Whatever do you mean?"

"Well, I, I just feel bad that we are being deceitful. I think you would be a wonderful husband."

"Ah, Bella, you know I love the company of men."

"I do know this, but I often dream of a fantasy world where we are together and you are my husband. Perhaps we were once husband and wife in another lifetime."

"Perhaps, I do have a fondness for you, but that is where my affection ends."

I leaned my head on his shoulder. "I know Manfri. I just think sometimes life can be unfair, almost cruel. I love Marcello with all of my heart and soul, but I still have these feelings of affection toward you, it confuses me at times, and I just wish . . . I wish that it could be different, is all."

"I understand," he told me as he kissed the top of my head. "Now let us go have that conversation with my parents.

Claire and Toni were just finishing up their practice for the new act. They bounced to the net and dismounted in front of the betrothed. "Hello children, how did it go at the parish house?"

"Very well, we must go back after the ceremony and sign the papers with our witnesses to make it official, and then Father Bovary will file it." He looked at me, his bride, and then at his parents. "Crystobella and I would like to have a serious conversation with the two of you, may we sit in the dressing area?"

"Of course," they agreed. Once everyone was settled in the dressing room his mother asked him, "What is so urgent?"

"Crystobella does not like deception and she wants to relate a story to you about recent events which led to our wedding being moved up."

They looked expectantly at Crystobella and she began. "I was recently in Versailles for a faire, my father, well, as you might have guessed, he drinks a bit. I went in search of him late at night because I needed him to help me with a matter about our horses. I had earlier in the day done a reading for a gajo, he was vile and rude, and he did not like what I had to say. He was a true shimulo! I knew my father would most likely be at a tavern, so I went into an alley which led to the kertsheema, the man appeared and called me a Gypsy whore. I tried to avoid him, yet, he attacked me from behind and raped me, which is why I am pregnant, and although I love your son, it is not his child. He has been man enough to offer his love and support and help me raise the child as his own."

They both looked aghast, yet Antonio said to her, "Our son learned his values from us and we shall do the same. We know it took courage for you to share this with us and we appreciate your honesty."

Claire came and gave me a hug. "What has become of this man? Will he cause future trouble?"

"No, I assure you he will not. My father and his companions made sure that he will not bother me or anyone else again. It is best if you do not know the details."

"I see," said Claire. "We will not need to speak of this again. All is going to be fine. We will love our grandchild no matter the circumstances through which he or she was delivered to us."

"Thank you, all three of you, I could not have married into a finer family."

Antonio produced some vino for him and his family and some grape juice which he poured for me. "A toast to the bride and groom! May you live a long, happy, and prosperous life!"

"A votre santé," the others said in unison.

"Darling would you accompany me to visit our witnesses?"

"Of course, Bella."

We walked first to Marcello's. I knocked on the door, but did not hear him inside. Just then we heard noises in the back of his cottage. We went to investigate. Marcello was working on a table and he had dropped his hammer to the ground making a clatter. "Hello, Marcello, we would like to discuss a matter with you, if you will."

"Of course, mi amor, I mean my friends." Manfri smiled at him.

I said, "You must be careful with your tongue my dear. After all, we are here to ask you to be a witness at our wedding."

"I should think that would be torture for me to watch as you marry another man."

"Yet, you know the truth of the matter and we need two witnesses we can trust, the other will be Giovanni, Manfri's lover."

"I expect I can endure it, if he can. We must keep up appearances, after all."

"Then it is settled." I shared the details with him. "We must go to Giovanni next, my love, and talk with him.

We will see you on Saturday, if not before." I gave him a hug and a kiss on both cheeks.

Manfri shook his hand and said, "Goodbye."

We walked to Giovanni's home. He lived in Mont Parnasse. "Your lover is wealthy; I presume from where he lives."

"Yes, he comes from a family that is considered upper class. They own the bolta I got our rings, or I guess, my ring at. His father is the gabori. Giovanni is the silver and goldsmith. He is quite good at design. That is why I wanted him to design my ring. He will have a similar design on his binak ring, so we shall always know and remember where our true love is pledged. He shall wear it on his right hand, of course."

"Great minds think alike, that is why I am using Marcello's grandmother's ring." We both laughed.

We knocked on the apartment door of Giovanni's parents' house. It was on Rue Delambre."

A housekeeper answered the door. After explaining we were here to see Giovanni, she said, "Master Giovanni is in his quarters. I will get him for you."

Giovanni showed surprise when he returned with the housekeeper. "What a wonderful surprise to see the happy couple," he said.

"We have come to ask a favour of you."

Please follow me into the sitting room. They all took a seat, Manfri holding Crystobella's hand as he could see the maid eavesdropping just beyond the doorway. "We would like it if you would be one of the witnesses in our nuptials this Saturday. What do you say, my dear friend?"

"I would be honored to do so."

We shared the details with him and told him, "It is late, we must go. I need to be home soon to rest as I have much wedding preparations to do," I added.

Manfri shook hands with Giovanni and winked at him as his back was to the maid. He whispered, "I will meet you at our rendezvous spot later tonight."

Giovanni said, "It was a pleasure to see you and I will see you again soon." It was his way of letting Manfri know the rendezvous was a go without speaking it out loud.

On the walk home I could not contain my excitement of meeting Giovanni. "He is so handsome and wealthy! It seems you have hit the jackpot with a beautiful wife and a gorgeous, rich lover on the side! What more could a man wish for?"

"Well, perhaps, marrying the person he loves."

"I agree, but I do love you, just as I am sure Giovanni will grow to love me. We have designed the perfect arrangement in which all parties can live happily ever after, even our parents."

"Yes, you are correct; fate has dealt us a good hand in that we can freely be with our partners of choice while avoiding ridicule. I am sure we would all be burned at the stake if the truth be told." He looked at Crystobella and she looked stricken. "What is wrong?" Manfri asked her.

"Please, never utter those words again! I am superstitious by nature and those words you spoke hit very close to the truth. If we are found out there will be dire consequences for all four of us."

"You are right, once more, I shall recant them."

I saw the shon was full and asked him if we may sit a moment and enjoy its splendor.

"Yes, we may, I am not meeting Giovanni until midnight."

"Why so late?"

"We must be ever so careful; you know the results of being discovered. Two men having sexual relations is the work of the devil in society's eyes."

"Yes, I know it well, I have the same consequences if I am accused of being a chovexani and Marcello has seizures, so they will burn him as well thinking he is my consort and I have possessed his soul. We all share this common bond, and we must pray that it is not that which fate has planned for us."

I once again lay my head on his shoulder and he put his arm around me. We looked like the young lovers we purported to be, yet appearances are often deceiving. I asked him, "Do you think that we have to consummate the marriage to make it legal?"

"Ah, I did not think about that. Since it is not a real marriage, possibly we will not. I should think we could go into our vurdon and spend the night after the ceremony so that people think we have consummated it."

"Yes, you are right."

Chapter Twenty

When we arrived back at the camp, there was a surprise waiting for us. My father had delivered on his promise of a new home for us. It was a bow-top, in poor condition, but it had potential. I loved it! My very own home! "Papa!" I exclaimed. "Thank you for this wonderful wedding gift!"

"Baby Bear, I want you and your husband to be happy, baxtalo. Part of this came from Antonio and is your cheiz. You must also thank him."

"We shall, Papa, Thank you."

"Let us look inside." We went in and took a look around.

I spoke first. "I see its potential and it will be the most admired vurdon when it is finished. We can hire Marcello to do the repairs . . ."

"Baby Bear, do you think that is wise?"

"Yes, father. Manfri and I have discussed this situation with Marcello and he understands completely. He knew that it was a paramitsha to believe I would be allowed to break with tradition and marry him. He has come to peace with my choice."

Manfri added, "He and I have spoken as well and he likes me, he has consented to be one of the witnesses in the wedding. I admire his integrity and his acceptance of that which fate has given us."

"I see you both are mature; this is a good thing when entering into a marriage."

"Thank you, Papa." I gave him a long hug, Manfri shook his vast, and they patted one another on the back, in that manly gesture of affection one often sees in the kertsheema.

"I must be on my way now; we are still perfecting our act for the upcoming cirque."

"Goodnight my future son-in-law."

I walked with him to the lane where I hugged him and kissed him goodbye. As he walked away, I waved and said, "Goodnight, my love!"

"Oh, Papa, I wish to start making my home cozy right away, but I am not feeling the best after such a long day. Perhaps we can sit by the fire and talk a bit? I would like to tell you about the beautiful dress Manfri's mother, Claire, is loaning me for the wedding."

We took our seats and talked for the next few hours until my sero began to nod. "I must sleep now, Papa Bear." I arose and Beau took that as his cue to follow me. I checked on my beloved horses and patted them goodnight. I lay down and was fast asleep before I could say my prayers. That night an intense dream came to me.

I was on the bed at Marcello's, I was naked; it was my wedding night. Manfri and Giovanni were there as well, we were all naked. I heard a voice as if it was disembodied say to us, "You must consummate your jekhipe; you are now all becoming one." I looked at my three suitors and beckoned them to the bed. I allowed them to pleasure me; I got on my knees, one was fondling my chuchis and passionately kissing me while entering me with his karbaro, another was behind me and he would slip his kar in just as the first left the void. The last was pleasuring the man behind me; they took turns thrusting their manhood within my mish. First from behind and then from the front as soon as one left me with an aching need, the other would fill it, the man in the back was receiving the other. Manfri, Giovanni, and Marcello would kiss one another as well as me. One of the men would climax and he would change places with another, the kisses made it such an intimate act. The men were spent and I wanted more! I loved all three of them, madly.

Chapter Twenty-One

I woke up in the morning feeling odd. What a streyino dream I had had. I was sure it was sent from the mulani, that vile mule would invade my dreams! I stepped outside and promptly vomited; *johai again*, I thought. I had been ignoring the mulani, hoping he would tire of tormenting me.

I heard him inside of my head. *"You think just because I am dead you are safe from me, but I am a mamioro and you will see my power very soon!"*

I began to cry and rushed to see my beloved. "Marcello! Are you here?"

He answered his door and ushered me in. "Mi amor, I had the most disgusting dream last night!"

"Me as well, it is the mulani! He has become stronger and more powerful; he must be drawing in the dark forces to help him. He threatened to make us ill; he said he was now a mamioro, a spirit or ghost who brings serious illness! He entered my thoughts and told me so. That is why I am here; I had to check on you!"

"Have you spoken with Manfri, did he and Giovanni have the same dream as well?"

"I do not know, my love. I came straight here." Beau began to growl and the hair on his back stood up. I felt a shiver down my spine. He is here! I feel his presence! We must put lon around the house and burn drab. "Begin saying the Lord's Prayer, Now!" We began in unison:

"Our father who art in heaven, hallowed be thy name thy will be done on earth as it is in heaven . . ."

I grabbed the salt from his cupboard and began pouring it around the house in a circle while still reciting the prayer. I went back adre of the house and pulled my herb bundle from my potchee, I lit it and began clearing the house. As I cleared, I recited a prayer of protection in Latin, it's strongest form... *"In nomine Padre, et filii, et espiritu sancti.... abbe male spiritus, abbe male spiritus . . .*When I finished with *"In Nomine Jesus Christi, Amen,"* Beau was calm and I felt the presence had vacated the house. I knew it was lurking outside in the shadows and I must have my guard up at all times.

I hugged Marcello. "Do you have your bujo with you?"

"Always, amor," he showed it to her.

"Good, Marcello, I love you so much, I could not bear it if anything happened to you."

"Nor I, you, mi amor."

We stood there a long while in that embrace until Beau brought us back to the present moment with a bark."

"There was a knock at the door and it startled them both. "Marcello asked, "Who is there?"

"It is I, Manfri and Giovanni is with me."

He opened the door and admitted the pair.

I did not need to ask by the looks on their faces, yet, I did. "You had the dream as well? Both of you?"

They nodded.

I began to explain the precautions they must take and told them they could follow me to my camp and I would bestow them both with bujos to protect them. I related what the ghost had told me. "He means us harm."

Marcello offered them a seat and a stout. They accepted.

"He is drawing power from the darkness; I believe that he is able to enter my dreams because I carry his seed, and as I am connected to each of you, he gains access to your dream world as well."

Giovanni gasped.

"Manfri, he did not know?"

Manfri shook his head.

I explained the situation to Giovanni. "We must make a united front that is more powerful than the darkness which backs him, whenever you are in a vulnerable place please recite the Lord's Prayer until you arrive to a place of safety. Does everyone understand what we are dealing with?"

They all nodded.

I said "We must go to my camp and get the bujos for you both. Marcello, will you come?"

"I will."

"We will tell my Papa that you have come to look at the vurdon and take measurements."

"Mi amor, what vurdon?"

"It is a gift from my father and Antonio for the wedding. It is in disrepair, yet, it has potential. I told my father you are okay with my choice of a husband and would repair it for us. That way he will not question you being around me or inside with me, it will give us more **Slobuzenja**. You are the best at woodworking, I know it will be a piece of art when you are done."

"That is a good plan, and luckily I agree with it."

Giovanni added, "I am an excellent designer, I shall help as well."

I replied, "Thank you, Giovanni, that is perfect."

"We must go now. Manfri and Giovanni, stay between Marcello and I as we have our bujos with us. I shall say the prayer of protection as we go to banish this mule!" She commanded her rikono "Beau on guard." We set out for my camp, taking the trail as it would be normal for the four of them to be seen together now. I recited the *Abbe Male Spiritus* under my breath as went.

Chapter Twenty-Two

When we arrived, I introduced Papa to Giovanni, then I asked him, "Do you have your bujo with you?"

"No, Baby Bear, why?"

"It is important you wear it for me father. I will explain later. I must get some for my shavora. Shall I bring yours out as well?"

"Yes, thank you, Bella."

I returned with my father's bujo and two others. "These hold strong medicine, they are magick, yet, you must keep them hidden to retain their protection and power." I handed one to each of the men.

Giovanni gave me a hug and said, "Thank you."

"Papa, good news! Marcello has agreed to fix the wagon. He is here to take measurements now."

Beau was calm, lying by the fireside and the horses where munching their hay. Just to be safe I poured the lon around the camp and burned some more herbs while praying. I circled each wagon and put a shield of protection around it as well as around my beloved horses.

We entered the vurdon. "You are our first official guests and it is fitting as you are familia, niamo!"

Manfri added, "We are a vista!"

I offered to get them some vino, but they declined. They all decided it is best to keep their wits about them. Giovanni is good with design and he offered suggestions to Marcello. They worked well as a team.

Marcello suggested to him, "Possibly you would like to join my woodworking business as a designer? We could charge an extra fee for your designs."

"I could use some supplementation to my income, I would love to join you." The two shook hands on it.

I believe the dream was meant to divide us, yet, it seemed to bring us closer. I commented on my thoughts and the men agreed. We retired to the yog, but soon it was time to sleep.

I bid my guests goodnight and told them, "Be safe on your journey home." I fell into bed and kept my bujo near; I put a crystal grid around myself and Beau to keep us safe in the night.

I awoke the following morning and all seemed well with the world. Claude was absent from his bunk and I knew he must be off womanizing. When I went outside, I saw my father slumped on the ground by the fire. I ran to him "Papa!"

I bent over him and checked for a pulse, he had one, it felt weak. I tried to rouse him, "Papa, where does it hurt?"

He groaned.

I tried to get him into a chair but it was too difficult for me to accomplish. I rolled him onto his back and checked his airway. It was clear. I decided to smack his face. He responded to me then. When he spoke, I could smell the alcohol on his breath. "Oh, Papa, you scared me! I thought the shimulo attacked you as he is now a powerful mamioro!"

"I only remember being by the fire and deciding to have a night cap before sleep, then I remember nothing, until you just slapped me in the face, Baby Bear." He rubbed his face for effect.

"I am sorry, Papa, I was afraid the mamioro had made you ill."

"I fear he did, Bella, but I will be okay."

"It is Thursday; we must be ready for the wedding by Friday night. Is there anyone that you wish me to invite?"

"Only the familyili of our kumpania."

"I will let everyone know when I go to secure the Rom Baro to perform the ceremony. What do you wish to eat for breakfast?"

"I think just a bit of bread, Baby Bear. I am not feeling well."

I brought it to him with an herbal chao. "Drink this; it will help you feel better. I will feed the horses and then Beau and I will be off on my rounds to gather the guests. I love you, Papa Bear."

I arrived at the Rom Baro's vurdon an hour later. I knocked on the side of the wagon. "Who is it?"

"It is I, Crystobella Franco. I have come to ask you to marry me and my betrothed."

"I charge one ècu, or six livres. Can you pay?"

"Of course, I can pay!"

He came outside to speak with me. "I will be there then to do the honors. Where and when?"

"It will be held in the cirque tserha of the familia de Gambian."

"The trapeze performers?"

"Yes, Manfri is my intended dom. Please be there by one o'clock in the afternoon. If you would, also please extend an invitation to all of the familiyi."

"Of course, it has been a pleasure doing business with you."

"Good day, sir." I continued to each campsite and extended my wedding invitation. Most of the manush consented as they knew a feast was to take place and there would be free drinks, every Gypsy loved free alcohol.

I was tired and feeling queasy once again, so I headed back to camp to take a nap, sov would serve me well.

My father came home in the evening and woke me. "Crystobella, the horses are not fed, and my supper is not made."

"Papa, I am ill, please can you make supper tonight?"

"You know that is your job, and besides it is good practice, who is going to take care of your child when you feel ill?"

Good old selfish Claude has returned, I thought. His generosity never lasts long. I drug myself from the bed and prepared him a meal. I was feeling a bit better and fed the horses and Beau as well. I patted Madeleine on the forehead and said, "Well my dearest we are both in the same boat. I am sorry if we made you work when you felt like this." The mare snuffled a bit and nuzzled my hand. I gave her a kiss and went over to the fire, taking a seat next to my father.

"What will you wear to give me away, Papa?"

"I shall wear my blue trousers and the fancy blouse I wore at my own wedding with a silk sash around my waist, and my best boots."

"Perhaps you could wear the bolo tie with the turquoise that grandmother gave you on your wedding?"

"If it will make you happy, then I will wear it, Bella."

"Thank you, Papa."

Marcello stopped by and joined us at the fire. He handed me a paper with some plans drawn on them. My father scooted closer so he could view them as well. "These are the plans that Giovanni and I came up with for your Vurdon. I can start on it tomorrow. "

"Marcello, these are wonderful! I love it!" I smiled at him.

"Giovanni has some ideas as how to decorate it and he will come by with fabric samples as well, it will be our wedding gift to you, the reconstruction, and decorating of your wagon. Of course, it will not be done by Saturday evening. Yet, it will be presentable for the newlyweds to stay in by then if you wish."

I jumped up and hugged Marcello; Claude could see that I still held great affection and love for him.

He thought, *she is sacrificing true love to please me, just as her mother had done for her own father.* Back then Claude had some wealth by Gypsy standards and he paid the highest bride price for Clara. She learned to love me, but it was not the great love that I tell to Crystobella that we held for one another. Clara almost despised me when I kept up my boozing and womanizing after the wedding. She even caught me with her cousin on our wedding night. I was ashamed to ever let my daughter find out the truth; for her mother died by her own hand rather than have to endure living with me one more minute. I wished I would have let my Bella marry Marcello, but the damage is done and it is too late now.

Marcello asked Claude, "Do you like the plans, sir?"

Coming back to the present Claude replied, "Yes, Marcello, they are good and you are a fine woodworker, I feel the vurdon will be a masterpiece, it will be the envy of all the Gypsies."

"Thank you, sir, you are too kind."

I told my father I was going to go inside with Marcello to allow him to measure for his improvements. Marcello and I slipped into the wagon.

Claude knocked on the door, "Baby Bear, I am going out for a bit, don't wait up."

"Sure, Papa," I leaned out of the doorway and gave him a kiss. "Goodnight."

I turned to my love. "Marcello! This means we are alone!" Beau made a noise, "Well, except for Beau," I laughed.

Her father looked back and saw the silhouettes in the window of her wagon in an embrace and he knew there was to be trouble ahead. He continued on, eager to drown his pain in the bottle and a wanton woman; preferably one with large chuchis.

Chapter Twenty-Three

"Mi amor, it is torture being so near you and having to pretend we are just friends."

"I feel the same, my love."

We embraced and tumbled to the bed, it was old, lumpy, and dusty, but neither of us seemed to notice. Before long we were naked and tangled together, one could not be distinguished from the other.

"I shall take you as my own amor," he thrust harder with every stroke.

I cried out, "I am yours, my love, take me."

He pushed hard into me and let out a growl. I felt his seed fill me and wrapped my legs around him, pumping furiously until I joined him in climaxing.

Later he lamented, "I must be going before anyone suspects what is really going on in here." He kissed me and gathered his things. Once he was dressed, he patted Beau on the head and strode from the wagon, I followed him with the dog on my heels. "Will you be all right alone, mi amor?"

"Yes, my love, I have Beau. He has grown into a fine handsome guardian."

Marcello looked down at the dog and saw he has indeed grown; he was large and strong and had a mean growl. He had no doubt he would protect her. "Goodnight, amor."

"Goodnight."

Chapter Twenty-Four

I lay in my bed and thought tomorrow is Friday already, only one day away from my wedding. My dress is beautiful and I am going to feel like a queen wearing it; the only thing that is missing is a groom that I love and adore. Not that I do not love Manfri, but in a platonic way. I made sure the grid was in place and patted my protector on the head before sleep overtook me.

True to his word Claude was not home when I awoke in the morning. I took care of the horses and was making breakfast, even though I felt a bit ill, I know must eat for the baby. I put some egg and sausage in Beau's dish and sat down with chao and a plate. Just then Marcello appeared with Giovanni. I invited them to join me.

They sat down and I offered, "I can cook for you, are either of you hungry?"

They both answered "No, just perhaps some café?"

I put some kafa on the fire and then turned my attention back to the men. Giovanni had some fabric samples to show me. They were magnificent.
"These fabrics look too expensive for my budget," I told him.

"It is my gift, choose what you like."

I squealed with delight and chose a few fabrics which were contrasting, yet, worked well together.

"Excellent choices," commented Giovanni.

Marcello had his tools and the wood was to be delivered any minute. Just then two men arrived with an open wagon full of wood. He went to help them unload it.

I needed to go into towne and see Manfri and his mother. I yelled to the men, "I need to go into towne for a bit, do either of you need anything?"

"Perhaps some ham and cheese with bread when you return for lunch." Marcello suggested.

Giovanni added, "And some pickle chutney, perhaps?"

"You will be eating the best ham and cheese for your efforts, as to the chutney, I may only be able to bring pickles . . ." I hugged each one of them good bye and was on my way with Beau following closely behind me.

I went directly to the tserha of the Gambians. "Hello, Claire, Manfri?"

Claire welcomed me in. "Please come to the sitting area. Everything is all set for tomorrow the decorators are set to arrive soon and the catering company will be here early in the morning. You can arrive any time after nine in the morning dear."

"Yes, I will. I must be sure that Manfri does not see me the day of the wedding, until I am escorted down the aisle."

"No, of course not. He will be doing last minute errands with his father. They have gone to the city centre to get fitted for their tuxedos and will have a guy's night out tonight. Does your father wish to join them; I can give him the address."

I Know Papa would be honored to be included, yet, he will not don a tuxedo, of that I am sure and I would prefer he stays close to home the night before so I can monitor his alcohol consumption as well as know where he is in the morning, he has a way of disappearing."

"Oh, yes, I understand."

"Is there anything I can assist you with today?"

"No, it is all set. I have a friend coming to help you with your hair and makeup tomorrow and I want you to have this." Claire pulled out a box with a ribbon around it from her skirt pocket. She handed it to Crystobella.

Inside was an exquisite crystal bottle of perfume. "It is beautiful; you did not have to do this. Thank you so much. It means a lot to me, as I do not have my dya here to share this special day."

"You are welcome, and I may not be your mother, but I will always treat you as if you are my daughter."

We embraced and I began to cry.
"Now, now, dear child, it is okay. Do not cry. Tomorrow is your day and it shall be magical."

"I cannot thank you enough. If you have nothing for me to assist you with, then I must be on my way. I promised Marcello and Giovanni to bring them lunch, they are renovating our Vurdon! Manfri and I will have a lover's nest to retreat to arter our nuptials. I would say to make you a grandchild, but that has already occurred!" We both laughed. I kissed my mother-in-law on each cheek. "See you in the morning!"

"Yes, dear, see you in the morning."

I went to the deli and bought some fine meat and cheese, then to the bakery to purchase some bread. I made sure to get enough for Claude and a treat for Beau, a nice kokalo. On the way home Beau's hair stood up on his back and he let out a low growl. I felt a maleficent force near me. I was glad I had my bujo and Beau, but I wished to get home all the same. I arrived a few minutes later, "Hello, dinner bell, hello!"

The two men emerged from the trailer. "Marcello spoke first. "We are famished, thank goodness you have arrived."

"Oh, pfhst, I am sure you would have survived a few moments more." I prepared their plates and made them some chao, chipping a bit of led from the block in the chest to cool it. We sat at the small table and ate together. I fed Beau bits under the table.

Claude strolled in during lunch. "Papa, I have some ham and cheese for dinner, are you hungry?" I always spoke of lunch as dinner and dinner as supper with Papa, as that is how Claude believed they were called.

"Maybe later, Baby Bear, I am not feeling well, I must lay down for a bit."

"Excuse me please, I must tend to my father." The men nodded their assent. I disappeared into my father's vurdon. "Papa, what seems to be ailing you?"

"I am weak and my pulse is threaded again. I felt dizzy and a bit queasy."

"Lay down, I will fetch a cloth and some cool pani nevi." I returned with the bowl and a cloth in a few moments, and began wiping his brow. "We must have you feeling better for the big day tomorrow, I have a bit of ginger tincture for you to try, and it is good for circulation and eases the stomach."

He took the tincture. "Do you have your bujo with you?"

"No, it is there, on the bedside table."

I looked for it, "Papa, it is not here! I began to search on the ground and found it under the edge of the bed.

"I felt the mamioro on my way home, he is waiting until we are weak, vulnerable, and you must be on guard at all times. Please keep this with you, I beg of you to do so." I put it in his hand and wrapped his fingers around it. "Promise me, Papa."

"I promise."

"Now I must go back and attend to our guests." I kissed him on the forehead, "Rest."

I grabbed three more bujos, securing one to Beau and the others to the horse's halters, "There, now we are all protected." I walked back to the men.

Marcello asked me to join them in the wagon to see the progress. "We feel you will be pleased."

Giovanni agreed. "Yes, you will not know it as the wagon you left this morning."

I peered inside. It took my breath away. Marcello had made a curved archway over the bed; it had enough room for the night stand and he had cut out stars in the intricate trim. It was ornate and reminiscent of a carousel. I squealed with delight. "Oh, it is more than I could ever have dreamed possible!" I threw my arms around Marcello and hugged him; before I realized what I was doing, I kissed him.

Giovanni cleared his throat. "I understand your gesture, yet, those in society will not look upon it with the insight I am privy to."

"Oh, yes, I lost myself in happiness, forgive me."

Giovanni continued, "It will be painted in gold, red, sage green, and yellow, with the main panels in royal blue. The pillows will be many and in shades of gold and sage, with a few red ones for accent. Marcello will build a mirror into the pattern behind the nightstand. I have the perfect antique oil lamp for the night stand as well, I shall bring a fine Persian rug for the floor and gold silk linens with a silk bed cover, red and embroidered in gold thread. "You and Manfri will be known as Gypsy royalty!"

A tear escaped my eye, and I hurriedly wiped it away. "You are so kind, both of you. I mean this situation is less than ideal and you are being so generous. After all, Giovanni, you should be sharing this with Manfri, not I. I should be sharing Marcello's cottage."

"It is okay my dear Crystobella, after all we want the best for the people we love, and I think I can speak for all of us when I say, we love one another. Besides I am sure we will all have our trysts in this fine love nest." He winked at her, "Now Marcello and I have much to do and will get back to work, you should check on your father."

I entered the vardo: "Papa, how are you feeling?"

"I am feeling better, Baby Bear. Thank you for your help."

"Perhaps you should visit the Doctor?"

"Nai, no need for that, my child, I will be okay. I must learn to curb my indulgence in drink and my lust for women.

I will be fine to walk you down the aisle tomorrow; do not worry your pretty little head."

"Yes, Papa, I look forward to seeing you in your splendid clothes, and it shall be a glorious moment when you hand me to my groom. Manfri is the perfect husband."

"He knew she did not really think that, but he said, "I am proud to call him my zhamutro!"

"I must tend to the horses now; let me know if you wish to have some ham and cheese, Papa."

I went out to the horses and brushed them, making sure their manes were combed and had ribbons in them. Ganache had healed well and Papa and I will enter the tserha upon their backs. After the ceremony I and my groom, Manfri, will leave on horseback, well, just until we are outside of the tersha, as the reception was to be held within it. I felt it was a grand entrance and exit, even if we would only ride out of the tent and walk back in. My beloved animals must be a part of the ceremony. Beau will be wearing a bowtie around his neck as well and shall be sitting beside me during the vows. I went to my table and sat down, I missed smoking my herbal cigarettes, yet, I must take care of the child within my womb. He already came from a bad seed and my love and care shall change his vile beginnings.

Chapter Twenty-Five

A few hours later the men emerged once more and asked me to come and look at the progress. I yelled to my Papa to join us. "I will come in a moment, Baby Bear."

Marcello helped me inside, Giovanni followed us, and my father came just as we got inside. It was small and a bit cramped with all of us inside but it was so beautiful that no one seemed to notice. The bed enclosure was on the back, against the wall to the right. On the left was a small area to sit and hang our clothing. There was also a place for a cradle, and a small wooden wall with an arch to enter through; inside was a bed for when the child grew. Giovanni told me, "I will hang some curtains in the arch with a beautiful silk tie to hold them back."

Marcello showed me a lid on the top of the bed which opened. I could keep baby supplies in there, and toys, and the other half of the top could have a mat put on it so I had a place to bathe and change the baby. He told me, "I am making the cradle for the child and it will be done before the arrival of the little angel."

On the wall to the left was a beautiful area that had just been tiled with teal blue tiles around the old cast iron wood-stove. Above it, Marcello had worked his magic with ornate shelves; one area was specifically for my herbs and spices. On the right side there was a beautiful bench with a built-in side table.

Giovanni said, "We will make a cushion for this bench and it will be covered in velvet, there will be many throw pillows and a chenille shawl to keep you warm in the chill."

"I can imagine it as it shall look when it is finished, and it will be magnificent! It is already so beautiful. I can help you paint it after the wedding."

Marcello firmly stated, "No, we will hire a painter, you must not over-do it with the child, and the fumes from the paint may make you faint. You are to worry about the cirque and month-long faire. After all, you must save up for the child; they need a lot of care and are expensive."

With tears streaming down my face, I hugged each of them and said, "I cannot ever repay this kindness, but I can cook your supper for you. Please come and sit by the yog as I prepare the food."

I looked in the icebox and found some leftover goose-meat. I put the popin in the bov and began to grill some vegetables. Papa brought out some lovina to share with the men. They were discussing the latest nevipe while they enjoyed their pibe. I enjoyed having familia around me; even if it was a rag-tag familia, not made of blood. I was proud to call this my familia. I only wished that Manfri and his parents could be here as well. *He will be tomorrow*, I thought, all of them will be, and it will be a celebration of love and life: as long as the mamioro stays away. I must remember to pour lon around the tserha and burn drab in the morning to ward off any mal intent and keep it at bay.

The group talked late into the night. I suggested they disband so they can rest before tomorrow's celebration.

"Yes, of course," said Marcello, "We were having such a nice evening we forgot the big event is only hours away."

I kissed Giovanni and Marcello on their cheeks and bade them farewell. "Papa, I must rest now, are you coming to bed?"

"In a bit, Baby Bear, I wanted to visit . . ."

"Aye! Papa, please not tonight, save it for tomorrow when we newlyweds will need our time alone, please?" She begged him.

"Okay," He acquiesced, and followed her into the vurdon.

It felt as if morning came too soon. "Papa, I must hurry to the tserha, I promised Claire to arrive by nine. Can you be sure to bring the horses to the ceremony?" I did not wait for his reply. "Be there two hours before we begin, the ceremony is at one. Papa, did you hear me?"

"Yes, Baby Bear, I heard you. You are good at giving orders, I believe you will be a fine monashay," he laughed.

"Oh, Papa!"

Chapter Twenty-Six

I called Beau and set off for my big day. I still felt uneasy as if there was a cloud of doom following me, but I would be strong and not let it affect me. This day was to be perfect and I shall not let a mulani interfere with my happiness today.

I entered the tent and it was like a dream, a Gypsy fairytale. There were flowers everywhere and small candles were set around the tent for later in the evening, and there was one on each table in a votive. Ribbons were strung all around, making it magical. It was durane svatura! I looked to the front of the tent and saw an arch, it was adorned with flowers, and there was a beautiful rug where my groom and I would stand for our vows.

"Yoo hoo, Crystobella!"

I turned to see Claire. "Good morning, Dya!"

Claire kissed her on the cheeks, "I am glad you feel this way, I shall do my best to honor that title."

"I hope the groom is behind the scenes, remember it is bad luck for him to see me before the ceremony."

"Yes, dear, do not worry. There shall be no gajengi baxt here!"

"I agree. Now what must I do first, Dya?"

"I will take you to the dressing room where the team of ladies in waiting shall transform you into the princess bride, and later after your vows you shall become a queen."

"Please, lead the way." We hooked arms and set off for the transformation room. My mother-in-law left me in very capable hands.

"Hello, love, I am Mary, and this is Chantelle', over there is Katie, and Jaunte'. We are your beauty designers." Everyone laughed at that.

"Jaunte' is the expert when it comes to face painting," the girls intoned.

She began by applying bismuth all over my face to give a light-reflecting sheen. She said, "I prefer to use pearl powder, but it is very expensive and I must substitute bismuth, often it is called tin-glass, because that is what it is made of. I know that it will give you that glow, although you are already glowing my dear, we shall enhance it for you."

"It is very parno, shall it make me look like a mulani?"

Jaunte' replied to her comment. "I can answer you when you tell me what you just said."

"I said the powder is very white, will it make me look like a ghost?"

Jaunte' laughed, "No. As I said before, it will give you a glow, the small pieces of glass, and tin ground up in the mixture will reflect light when it shines on your face. You will be beautiful, do not worry."

Chantelle' worked on her hair, adding oils and combing it, while the other two women were massaging her feet. "I have never been so pampered in all of my life," I told the women.

"It is your wedding day and all women should be pampered on their wedding day," said Mary. They all agreed, nodding their heads in unison.

The day was filled with chit-chat and laughter. I was enjoying this immensely.

I looked into a mirror, my cheeks had a slight pink glow, and I was told by Jaunte', "I used a bit of ground up alabaster, mixed with rose water, lemon juice, and a touch of red vermillion, and on your lips we put carmine, they look like rubies. Now for the eyes!"

I could see Jaunte' loved her job. She snatched away the mirror and told me, "look up and keep your eyelids closed, please." I obeyed. After combing and grooming my eyebrows, she applied a bit of wax with kohl to hold them in place and said, "Now I will apply a slight blue to your lids and then accent the eye by putting kohl around the lash line, I know it is not common in society to accent the eyes but all of the actresses do it to bring out their eyes."

"Actually, we Gypsy women have been applying kohl for ages, it is quite common in Asia, and Egypt, it has been used in our culture for generations," I informed them.

"Oh, interesting," said Jaunte'. I wish I was Egyptian."

"Well, Gypsies are not actually from Egypt, we are just called Gypsies because people assume we came from Egypt. Mostly we are from India and Eastern Europe, although we can be from anywhere; we are a familiyi of travellers, and not necessarily related by geographical location or blood."

"Kate said, "Wow, I never knew all of the facts about Gypsies, we often hear you are witches, tramps, and thieves, people to be feared, yet, you are intelligent and have a rich cultural history. Thank you for sharing it with us Crystobella."

"My pleasure. I often am saddened by how people treat us, yet, there are some bands that have become what they are accused of because that was what was expected of them. Circumstance shaped their fate. Most of us have been taught the old ways, those of the ancients. We like to have a strong, pure heart and live by the law of nature; harm none, no one. I feel that we are a much-misunderstood culture."

The women agreed. They once again produced a mirror for her to peer into.

I could not believe the face staring back at me was my own. I looked exactly like my mother, just as beautiful, if not more. I felt as if I would cry and asked for a handkerchief.

"No, no, you mustn't cry! You will destroy all of our work!" Jaunte' chastised.

"Oh, of course, I am sorry, I will cry on the inside." This elicited laughs from the group once more.

"Now to finish your hair," said Chantelle'.

"Bal is the Romani word for hair," I told them.

"I shall now finish your bal," said Chantelle'. She had Crystobella look straight ahead as she teased and puffed her hair. With ringlets falling around her face, yet, she left the top flat; as was the custom. She placed a very beautiful crown around her head with a jewel that hung down on the forehead. Then the women helped her get into her gown. She looked so stunning that she actually gasped when she peered into the mirror once more.

"I cannot thank you enough," If you come to the cirque and faire, stop by my stall at the market where I will have set up an ofisa. I will gift you with a bujo, a medicine pouch to protect you or give you a reading; your choice."

The women giggled and said they would be pleased to accept her gifts. "See you next week then earth angel," said Jaunte'.

I realized Jaunte' had the gift of sight.

It was now noon. *I must find my father*, I thought. I went out to the main area. I called for my father, "Papa, Papa!"

To my horror Manfri turned and saw me! I ran from the tent, directly into my father's arms. Frantically I told him, "Papa, he saw me, it is gajengi baxt! We are cursed!"

"Now, now, Baby Bear; please do not give power to such non-sense. We are not cursed. After all, this is only a superstition. It will all be well. Please calm down, try to enjoy your day."

"Yes, Papa, you are right." I took a deep breath. "Where are the horses, the groi?"

"I have put them in the stanya behind the tserha. They are being watched over by the grooms. All is well, Bella."

"Yes, I know Papa, yet, I have this sense of foreboding that has been attached to me for weeks now, I cannot seem to lose it."

"You are dwelling on that gajo, the mulla will never be found, it is done. We must move forward Bella, please focus your thoughts on the present."

He did not want to let her know the constable was in towne asking people for information on the disappearance of the shimulo. He feared the worst, yet, did not want to alarm his daughter. "You are pakvora, my Baby Bear." He went adre to speak with his zhamutro. "Manfri! I must speak with you! Manfri?"

"I am here, Claude, near the altar; I felt the need to say a prayer for today. Then I saw Crystobella, she looked stricken and I did not know what to do. I wanted to go to her, yet, I knew she fears me seeing her today, and she would have run from me, she did run from me!"

"Yes, she is very sensitive and believes in superstition. I tried to talk some sense into her; she is convinced there is a curse upon us."

"Yes, I feel it as well, there is a sense of dread that I cannot leave behind. I feel as if fate is catching up to us and it is a prikaza."

"Manfri, please focus your thoughts on the good in your life, like I have asked of Bella. We shall not speak again of this non-sense, no more talk of prikasa or dread, I mang of you, please zhamutro."

"Yes, I shall look towards the good in my life, thank you sastro."

The two men embraced and as Claude turned to leave the Rom Baro arrived. He was a large man with mischief in his eyes, and he had thick brows giving him a stern look, his voice was gruff and he barked, "Are we having a ceremony or not?"

Manfri answered him, "Yes, Rom Baro. We shall begin in a half an hour."

"Why then, did the chavi insist I be here by noon?"

"Well, if that is the case, then you are late. Perhaps this is the reason she asked you to arrive an hour early."

Manfri asked, "Shall we find my dya and let her give you the details of the ceremony?"

"Yes, lead the way," he barked again.

Manfri left the Rom Baro with his mother and went to get his tuxedo on. He found Marcello and Giovanni in the dressing room; they were wearing their finest clothing: Marcello had an Italian suit and Giovanni, well; of course, he owned a tuxedo, so he was dressed similar to the groom.

"Hello Gentlemen, are we ready to get this shindig going?"

"It is the groom! Hello, you handsome devil," said Giovanni.

Marcello said, "Glad to see you, my friend."

Chapter Twenty-Seven

"Yes, we are ready," the men told him. They walked out to the main floor and took their places; many of the guests had arrived and were seated according to their acquaintance with the bori or the kirvi; the gruff Rom Baro stood at the altar, ready to begin.

"If I had to guess, I would say the Rom Baro is anxious to get to the food, he looks like a xari!" The men laughed. The Rom Baro gave them a stern look.

Soon the music began and Manfri's mother was escorted to her seat by his father, who sat beside her. She looked stunning in a sage green silk gown adorned with crystals. Then the music changed; the tent flaps opened to reveal Crystobella and Claude perched atop their horses. They were grand! The horses had flowing ribbons and Crystobella was a sight that could make men faint, and women become envious. Manfri for a moment wished the wedding were real, as well, and then he caught himself. He heard Marcello take in a sharp breath and remembered the reality of what they were doing.

The horses slowly pranced to the front of the tent where grooms took them back out after Claude helped Crystobella from her steed. He escorted her to her kirvi and the Rom Baro began the ceremony.

"Who gives this bori in marriage?"

"It is I, her father."

He looked at Crystobella and continued, "Kasko san?"

"I am the daughter of Claude Franco."

He instructed Claude, "Please give her vast in marriage to the zhamutro."

Manfri and Crystobella joined hands and faced one another. Manfri could feel her trembling and squeezed her hands to reassure her, it was okay.

The Rom Baro asked, "Manfri, do you accept Crystobella as your monashay? Will you pakiv, dav pakiv Crystobella? Will you keep her for all time and forsake all others, as long as you both shall live?"

Manfri replied, "I take Crystobella for eternity as my monashay."

He looked to Crystobella. "Do you accept Manfri as your dom? Will you Pakiv, dav pakiv Manfri? Will you keep him for all time and forsake all others, as long as you both shall live?"

I replied, "I take Manfri for eternity as my dom."

The parent's responded in unison, "Bater!"

"May the Ray Baro look down upon you both with favour and bestow a lifetime of love to your union. Yekhipe!" Intoned the Rom Baro.

Please produce the angustris and the galbi for a blessing. Marcello handed the rings to the Rom Baro and Giovanni handed over the two gold coins. The Rom Baro said a blessing in Romanes and passed his hands over the items three times before handing them to the kirvi and bori.

I looked down at my rikono, Beau. He was sitting patiently at my side and looking up at me; I took a moment to pat his head, and everyone laughed. The Rom Baro asked us to exchange the sacred symbols and to place the rings on the left hands of their chosen one. They did so. "Now place your coin in your spouse's hand and fold your fingers over it."

He looked to the xanimiki asking them to join the kirvi and bori. They came to the altar, he handed them a gilded piece of rope and asked them to bind their children together as a family. The parents took turns wrapping the golden rope around the pair. The Rom Baro excused them. He intoned, "What Ray Baro has bound together let no one chin asunder.

He removed the gilded rope and told Manfri, "You may now place the dicklo on her head, he handed a delicate headscarf to him, and it was adorned just as her gorgeous gown was. Manfri placed it gently on her head. He asked Crystobella once more, "Kasko San?"

I replied, "I am buino to be the Romni of Manfri Gambian."

"Manfri you may kiss your wife!"

Would the xanamiki please come to the altar once more and bring the pliashka and make the first toast to lashav honor the familia.

Antonio opened the bottle and poured a shot into each of the five small glasses sitting on the table beside the altar, offering one to each of the new members in the familia. "Here is to the new wortacha, the union has created a new vista! Sastimos!" Everyone clapped and the familia drank their first toast together.

The Rom Baro asked the couple to face the guests. "In yekhipe, I present to you, Mr. and Mrs. Manfri Gambian!"

The natsiyi, niamo, and other esteemed guests stood and cheered for the new couple. The horse groom led the horses back into the tent and the couple mounted them, Crystobella sitting side-saddle was lifted by Manfri onto the Zen and they galloped out hand in hand.

When we were a safe distance from the tent, we dismounted and led the horses back to the Stanya area. Handing the reins to the grooms; we called Beau and went back to the tserha. Upon our entrance the guests cheered and immediately chanted, kiss, kiss, kiss . . . we obliged.

Manfri announced, "The rahat lokum of the abiav would be served now and immediately after we xa, we will enjoy the rovliako khelipen, followed by glasso for all of the guests to enjoy. Of course, there will be pibes flowing like a river, please enjoy yourselves!"

We, the newlywed couple, took our places at the familia table. We continued to drink the rum. Although I had pretended to drink mine and was still doing so, the rest of the familia were becoming quite jolly. Marcello and Giovanni were seated with the family as they were the witnesses.

Antonio began to tease his son, "Soon it will be time for zheita!"

"Papa, please," he begged.

But the slightly drunk companions began to tease him, "You will need much strength for your honeymoon night! If you drink too much you may not get a porado!"

"Please, my monashay is present! Show some barearav and watch your cheebs." He asked Crystobella to accompany him outside to gaze at the shon. He held her arm as they went outside.

I told him I was a bit cold and he placed his jacket over my shoulders. I leaned against him as he said, "I am sorry for my father he has a lose cheeb when he has been indulging in drink. My mother is very forgiving."

I gazed into his eyes and I felt an overwhelming love for this man. I leaned in and kissed him hard. Marcello had just walked up, "What are you doing?"

"Marcello, I ummm, I was just keeping up appearances."

"It looked like more than keeping up appearances, mi amor."

"I am sorry. I was confused for a moment. He is so kind to me and with the ceremony, I just forgot my place."

"Marcello, I assure you, you have nothing to fear from me, I am in love with Giovanni. I was as surprised as you are."

Marcello stepped closer to her, "Do you love him?"

"Marcello, you are my one true love, I do love Manfri, but as a phal, a brother. Marce' forgive me."

He strode closer to her and Manfri excused himself. Marcello took me into his arms and kissed me with such force I knew he was claiming me for all of eternity, and I knew that there would be no other man for me, ever. I had felt confused with Manfri as the ceremony was so real, but now I began to kiss him back. "I will always love you," I gasped as I kissed him again.

"And I you . . ."

"Crystobella!" Her father's voice broke them apart. Has the beng gotten a hold of you? What are you thinking? I guess you are your father's child after all!" He stomped off.

I called after him "Father, whatever do you mean? Please father . . ." but he had gone.

We should get back inside.
I saw Manfri at the wedding familia table. I joined him and Marcello went to get some food. I whispered into my husband's ear, "Please forgive me?"

"You are forgiven; soon it will be time to share our wedding dessert, the mariki. Now, besh, darling." I sat down beside my husband.

His mother addressed the guests. It is now time for the couple to share their wedding dessert. They chose mariki. For those of you who are not of Romani descent it is a sweet, layered, pizza-shaped pastry from flour, powdered milk, sugar, and bread, enoy!

Manfri fed a piece to me and I did the same for him, the manush cheered and clapped. It was now time for the rovliako khelipen. I was thankful that we did not have to participate in it and only had to watch the performers dance. After the performance they Gypsy melodies began and my husband and I took our first dance as dom and romni. It was slow and had a haunting melody. I got through it and told Manfri, "I need to sit down, I am feeling faint." He ushered me to the table.

I asked my new dom, "How soon would it be acceptable to leave?"

He replied, "I should think in an hour's time we could sneak away."

"Could you alert Marcello and Giovanni that we should all convene at Marcello's cottage tonight? He has a spare room so you and Giovanni can stay there and he and I can be together in his room."

"Well, yes, but what about your father, won't he be suspicious if we do not go to our vardo?"

"I believe he might, although I expect he will not be returning home tonight. I also think he already knows the truth."

"I will spread the word."

I saw him speak to the other two men and knew that all was set for tonight. It would be easier to meet and go to the parish house to sign the paper tomorrow. The hour flew by and Manfri stood up to announce that he and his wife were to retire for the night.

Everyone cheered sastimos and wished us well.

I knew that Marcello had left much earlier and Giovanni would come in about an hour's time. We called to Beau and set off for the cottage in the woods.

"If anyone sees us and asks, we will say Marcello loaned us his cottage as our vardo is not completely finished."

"That is a good plan Crystobella."

I felt his tension and she said, "You are angry at me for kissing you, yes?"

"Of course, I am. The thing is, I rather enjoyed it, and that caught me off guard. I mean, I love men, I love Giovanni, but you stirred something within me."

"I feel the same way. Perhaps we are connected by fate, by another lifetime?"

"Perhaps."

Chapter Twenty-Eight

We arrived at the cottage and Marcello let us in. As soon as he closed the door, he gathered me into his arms. "Mi amor, I am so glad to be able to hold you. It was torture seeing you and Manfri together all evening. It should have been us."

Manfri said, "I am sure Giovanni feels the same, Marcello."

"Yes, it was hard for all of us, my love," I added. "Marcello, shall we retire to your room?"

"Yes, of course."

"Manfri said, "Goodnight, I will let Giovanni in, but Marcello, can you show me to our room, please"

"Oh, yes, forgive me. I am much stressed tonight it seems." He led Manfri to the room opposite his, "there you are; everything you need should be inside. Goodnight."

"Sweet dreams, you two."

"And to you."

Marcello was so happy to have his beloved with him that he nearly damaged her dress helping her out of it. "Please be careful, my love. This dress belongs to Claire, Manfri's mother."

"Yes, of course, I will be careful. Or perhaps you would like Manfri to remove it?"

"Marcello, please! I will not tolerate this type of behavior. You are the one I love. I cannot help but have feelings for the man I married. He is like a pral to me. I was caught up in the moment and imagined it was you I was under the moonlight with . . . can you please let it be?"

"Yes, I can." He grabbed me and tossed me onto the bed, covering me as if he were a stallion. We fell asleep soon after."

Giovanni arrived later on and Manfri let him in, shutting and locking the door just in case. "My lover, I thought we would never be together tonight. Thanks to Crystobella we have the perfect get away." He pulled him into his arms and began to kiss him passionately. They stumbled to their room where they fell on the bed, nearly tearing one another's clothes off. They fell asleep unclothed in each other's arms.

The next morning, I was the first up, I needed to go outside and vomit; my morning sickness was easing, yet, after last night's food and drama, it flared up. I returned and began cooking for the men. They straggled in one by one, and asked for café. "I will prepare the kafa soon," I said. I served them their food and went to the stove and filled the djezbeh. I set it on the stove top and returned to the table with my chao.

"Giovanni asked, "What is it I am eating?"

"Saviako and bokoli, it is Beau's favorite," I teased the men.

The kafa was soon done and the aroma filled the kitchen, I served each of them, beginning with Marcello so as not to anger him again. The men seemed to perk up after their second cup.

I reminded them, "We shall need to be ready soon to go to the church."

We went ando foro around two in the afternoon. We began the walk to the parish with Beau close at my side. I was feeling uneasy once more. "Is anyone else feeling a chill, like there is an amirya over us?"

Giovanni replied, "I do not know what an amirya is, Crystobella, so I do not know if I feel one."

Manfri and Marcelo both agreed there was an odd feel to the air. Beau was growling low in his throat and his hair was standing up on his ruff.

"Everyone has their bujos, yes?"

Everyone said, "Yes."

We arrived at the parish and the housekeeper answered the door. She led us to the office where Father Bovary was seated. "Come in, please, come in."

"Manfri took the lead, "We are here to sign our marriage registry."

"Of course, of course." He took it from the top drawer of his desk. "Here you go."

Each one took their turn at signing the paper. Father Bovary told the group, "It is now official! You are registered and recorded. He Shook the groom's hand and told the bride congratulations.

They bid him adieux, and went to the café.

I inquired of the men, "You are having more kafa?"

"Why yes," said Giovanni, "it is the best cure after a wild night at a party."

"No, my drarnego is the best cure for whatever ails you."

There was a long moment of silence and I spoke first, "Do you all realize that tomorrow is the first day of the Lafayette Cirque and month long Reveller's Faire?"

Manfri responded, "I know, it has been a busy week, but now with the wedding behind us and our practice perfected, I think the Gambian's are ready!"

"What about me?" I responded.

"You are a Gambian now, are you not?"

I giggled, "Oh yes I forgot!" I thought a moment and said, "I am almost ready as well, it is good that the wedding is behind us and we can focus on the faire."

Beau barked and I added, "Beau agrees!"

Marcello said, "Yes, I am to have a tent at the market to sell my woodwork, I have quite a collection to show."

Giovanni said, "My father and I also have a place to sell our jewelry, it is in the main buildings that are frequented by the aristocratic citizens."

Manfri teased his lover, "Ooh la la, you are special Giovanni, do you think you might have time to visit the rest of us commoners?"

"Manfri, you speak in jest! I will sneak away anytime my father turns his back!"

Manfri looked at his companions. "I think we shall all be going about our business now; I must get my last practice in tonight with my parents. And you my wife?"

"I shall need to go to the kumpania and finish the bujos and herbal remedies, so I am ready in the morning to set up my ofisa. I must also wash the outfits that I will wear as it will be a long month and I will have to rotate them."

Giovanni told them, "I have to be at a family dinner, my mother insists every Sunday that we meet as a family and break bread."

I said, "That is a beautiful tradition. I think that the four of us should meet every Saturday for our familia feast, it can be our new tradition!"

The group agreed. They made a pact to meet every Saturday from now forward.

Manfri bid farewell to his shavora, kissing his romni on the sero as he winked at Giovanni. He said, "Darling, I shall see you in the evening at our vardo, try to make it cozy!"

I replied, "I shall my dom!"

Giovanni left to go to dinner and Marcello said, "I shall walk you home if that is okay with your husband."

Manfri gave his consent and we went their separate ways.

Chapter Twenty-Nine

On the walk home I got the chills.

Marcello asked, "Are you all right?"

"I still feel the presence of the Mamioro; I feel it is getting stronger. I have a sense of foreboding that is always with me now."

"It shall be okay, mi amor, all will work out for the best, you shall see. Please do not worry."

"Yes, I hope you are correct, Marcello, and it is just my nerves with the child and stress."

Beau ran ahead of me and got to camp before Marcello and I. He was waiting by his food dish as if to say he was starving. "Look at him! He must be famished!" I looked to Marcello, "I shall get him some food and feed the horses, would you like anything?"

"I would love a glass of your famous herbed tea, and maybe a bit of the bread and cheese if there is any about."

"Of course, I shall serve you the tea now and the food after I tend to my brood."

He loved to watch her as she worked, she took such great care of the animals, the same way she took care of people. She had a good heart and he was blessed to have her in his life.

I returned shortly with his food and took a seat beside him. "Here you are, bon appétit!"

He took the plate and I began to get the fire started. "Mi amor, please, allow me to do that after I finished my bite."

"But if Papa comes, he will demand his supper."

"Then he shall wait!"

I did not want to argue the point and sat in silence with him while he ate. When he was finished, true to his word, he arose and took some wood from the pile and began to get the fire going. He told her, "You could get the supplies for supper if you wish; the fire shall be hot soon."

I returned with the supplies I needed and began to prepare sarma. "Marcello, you may stay for supper if you wish, it takes some time to prepare, so you may be hungry again by that time."

He told her, "Actually, I was going to do a bit of work on the vardo for you, so that would be lovely if I could join you for supper after I am finished."

My father strolled in about thirty minutes after Marcello went inside the vardo. "Crystobella!"

"Yes, Papa, I am here. I am getting supper ready."

"Good, what are we having tonight?"

"Stuffed cabbage. I know it is one of your favorites."

"Yes, normally it is, yet, I am feeling like eating mas and potatoes tonight."

Marcello could hear him bellowing and came out to see what the ruckus was about. "What is going on out here? I could hear you inside the vardo."

Claude turned to him, obviously drunk and pointed at his daughter; she refuses to make me meat and potatoes!"

Marcello calmly said, "Crystobella, please make some kafa for your papa." He looked Claude in the eye and said, "You shall be happy to eat whatever she has made for you. You are lucky that she is still here, after all, she is now married and should be with her husband and his family, count your blessings."

"You should also, remem . . . mem . . . member she is married as well!" Claude slurred the words at him.

"I am aware of her marital status, sir." He turned and went back into the vurdon to work.

I handed my father his kafa and helped him to sit in a chair. "Papa, enjoy your pibe, and I will have your plate ready soon." I went back to the fire and cooking.

Claude began to torment me with his words, "You are just like me! Your mother despised me and she took her own life rather than live with me, she must have known you were the same bad blood, she left you behind as well . . ."

I gasped and dropped the spoon I was filling the cabbage with, "Papa, please say it is not true! Say it is the drink talking, that you are just being mean!"

"It is true, I was a man who loved women and booze, she caught me with her cousin on our wedding night, with my pants down, you might say, after that she tried to love me, but she truly despised me and you, you are just like me, she knew! I saw you and Marcello on your wedding night as well, you have bad blood . . ."

Marcello came out and hit Claude hard, knocking him from his chair. "She is nothing like you! You will never defile her character again, or I shall kill you, do you understand Claude? What you saw was her comforting me as I told her how much I loved her and how it was tearing me apart to see her marry another man. She is kind and loyal and she will not betray Manfri. Now apologize to her!"

I was standing there stunned and I saw my father look to me and back at Marcello, before he spoke. "I am sorry Baby Bear; can you forgive me?"

"Yes, Papa." I went back to preparing his food with tears streaming down my face.

Marcello helped her father up and told him, "I shall share this news with Manfri and if you do not show her respect, you will lose her, I will let them camp on my land in the wood. You can get your own plate of food."

He went to Crystobella and put his arms around her, "It is okay darling. You are not like him. You will stop catering to his every need and let him be a man, let him take care of himself and stop bullying you around. Now, let's get your things ready for tomorrow, we can wait here for Manfri, and then you both can stay at my cottage again tonight. You need rest before the long month of work."

"Thank you, Marcello, but I feel that we should stay here, after all it is our home now."

"We shall talk with Manfri and see what he thinks best, okay?"

I agreed with him and began preparing my wares and he went back to work inside the vardo. He called to me a bit later, "Bella, come here please, have a look."

I peeked inside, the bed area was painted, and there was a perina on the bed with Sherandas scattered about the bed. Beau's bed was put beside my bed as well. I threw my arms around Marcello's neck and kissed him, "I love it! Thank you so much!"

"It is my pleasure!" I must be going now, are you sure you do not wish me to wait for Manfri and see if he would prefer staying at my house?"

"We must learn to deal with Papa as a couple, and I am very distraught with his news, I am hoping after he eats and sobers up, he will explain his revelations to me."

"Then I shall take my leave, you know where to find me if you change your mind or need me in anyway." He kissed the top of my head and walked towards the wood. Just past the entrance to the camp he encountered Manfri. "I would like to share what happened between Claude and Crystobella at camp tonight." He told Manfri the sorted story and added, "Claude is drunk and I have extended an offer of my house for you and she tonight if need be. Please tread carefully with him tonight, I have already knocked him down myself once."

"Thank you, Marcello. I shall use the utmost caution where he is concerned." He shook his hand and said, "Thank you for your kind offer."

Chapter Thirty

Manfri saw Crystobella by the fire, she was weeping, and Claude was nowhere to be seen. "My darling wife, where is your father, and what has he done to you?"

"I was moving some of my things into our vardo for the night, and he just left."

"Normally this is a good thing. Why are you upset by it this evening?"

"Because he told me a revelation about, he and my mother, and he said she was killed by her own hand because she despised him and knew I was his, we had bad blood, so she left us."

"Crystobella, I am so sorry, I am sure he was just drunk, it cannot be true. You are nothing like Claude. You are good and just. Come here." He took her in his arms and held her as he gently rocked her, she dozed off in his arms by the fire; and he carried her inside the vardo. He was amazed at the beauty of the bed as he laid her on it. Beau curled up in his own bed. Manfri thought he would be sleeping on the bench, yet it was not finished, so he crawled into the bed with his romni. He held her close and fell sound to sleep.

I awoke and found myself wrapped in Manfri's arms. *What is this?* I thought. *Oh no, did we . . .* I could not remember the night; it was all fuzzy in my head. Manfri began to stir and I tried to slip out from his embrace.

He opened his eyes, "Good morning, sweet angel, how are you feeling?"

"Manfri, did we . . .?"

"Oh, nai, heaven's no! You were in such distress last night I held you to comfort you and you fell asleep in my arms. You told me that your papa shared some terrible news with you."

"Oh, yes!" It all came flooding back to me now. "He told me my mother would rather be dead than stay and take care of me; he said I am just like him because he saw me kiss Marcello at the abiav. He doesn't understand."

"My dear, he was drunk, I am sure he was just trying to hurt you. You know that your heart is zuhno, I know that your heart is pure, and so does anyone that meets you. He is miserable and wishes all of us to feel as he does. Pay him no mind, Bella."

"You are correct. I will try to let it go. It most likely is the mamioro trying to tear us apart, as we are weaker when we are not united." I kissed him on the cheek and bounded from the bed, "I must let Beau out and relieve myself."

He joined her at the edge of the wood. He said to her, "I never thought you, I and Beau would be xin, uh, be urinating together."

This made me laugh heartily.

"I shall get you some breakfast after I tend to the horses. What would you like, husband?"

"Some of your saviako, I found it to taste amazing!"

I told him lucky for you I have the pastry premade; I popped a few in the oven to warm. And he had some herbal chao by the fire as they warmed.

I went to take care of the horses. I peeked inside of my father's vurdon and saw that he was not there; probably for the best. I returned to the campfire and prepared our plates, joining Manfri.

He handed me a chao. "I am sure you must go soon, and so must I. Shall we pack and head into towne after we finish taking our breakfast?"

"Yes, we shall; Beau!" He whistled and Beau came running, he had grown into a grand dog. "Bella, our hairy son has become quite a handsome man!"

I giggled and said, "Why, yes, he has."

We set off on the lugo drom to towne. When we arrived at the Gambian's tserha, I handed him a pail. "Here is lunch; it is a bit of xaritsa and fusui eski zumi."

He kissed her cheek, "My favorite! I shall need to watch my weight with a wife who can cook! The trapeze shall bend if I become fat!"

I smacked his arm playfully; have a great day and I will be back this evening for the show after I close my ofisa. Give your parents my love."

Chapter Thirty-One

I went to the other side of the faire grounds. Once the ofisa was set up I stood back to have a look and see if it needed any changes. I heard a male voice behind me say, "It is magnificent; I do not think I could have done better!"

"Giovanni, how nice to see you," I kissed each of his cheeks.

"Have you escaped from your father so soon? Or perhaps you have not arrived yet?"

"He has sent me on an errand to fetch some of our pieces he had forgotten. I shall return later. Is there anything I could bring for you from towne?"

"I am fine, thank you. Please stop back whenever you have a moment. It is always good to see you." He nodded and went on his way.

I looked back at my ofisa, it was magnificent. I should do well today. I donned my dicklo and painted my eyes with kohl and made my lips lolo using some mashed herbs and alcohol. Now I looked the part. I sat down at my table with the crystal ball in front of me and when I looked up, I had my first customer gazing at me.

"Hallo, what may I do for you? A reading from the cards? Gazing into the crystal ball, or perhaps a bujo, crystal, or herbs?"

"I am with the police, Constable Donner, ma'am. We were alerted to the disappearance of a man in Versailles some months ago, I was told he had come to see you the day he went missing."

"Yes, but I told Constable Conrad everything I know. The man did not like what the cards had to say and he spat on my table and left. That is the last I saw of him."

"Yes, ma'am, well thank you. If he should show up here could you please tell him we are looking for him?"

"Yes, I will Constable, but I heard that he had runoff with another woman, you know how people talk."

"That seems to be the general consensus, ma'am. We must be thorough in our investigation whenever a person has gone missing. You have been of particular interest as someone saw his wife visit you the next day; that piqued our interest."

"Yes, she did, I did not know at the time that she was his wife, it was not until later when her sister came here to tell me that he had run off and her sister was now happily married to a nice man and wanted to thank me for my advice."

I continued, as I talk when I am nervous. "On that day, I simply told her that I could see her husband and he was with other women, he seemed to like her money and if she followed her heart prosperity and love would come to her. She thanked me and left. At that time, I did not know who she was married to."

"It seems that the advice you gave her was generic enough. Why, may I ask did her sister show up here?"

"She was attending an aristocratic ball near here and she wanted to deliver a message from her sister and have a reading of her own, as she was unlucky in love. I advised her to do the same as her sister, follow her heart."

"Thank you again, ma'am, and please let us know if he contacts you."

"I will, but I am sure he has no reason to, he did not like what I had to say to him."

"And what was that, might I ask?"

"That he must change his ways and stop boozing and womanizing if he wanted to be happy and prosper."

"Well a man like that would probably not like, nor heed that advice, again, good day." He walked away and wandered around the faire.

I knew the mamioro, vile shimulo, sent the shanglo here to upset me before I began, but he would not win. I took a few deep breathes and patted Beau under the table. Soon a woman came and sat in front of me, she asked for a crystal ball reading and bought some drab, many more were to follow. By evening I felt as if I had been dragged behind a carriage! I closed my ofisa and went to the tserha of the Gambians.

I entered from the back near the stanya. "Familia? Hallo!"

Claire greeted me with a kiss on both cheeks. "Hello my darling, have you come to see the show?"

"Yes, I am excited! Is it all right if Beau stays here in the dressing area?"

"Yes, dear, you can have a seat in the front row, the roped off area for our VIP guests."

"Thank you, Dya."

"Yes, dear, enjoy the show." I will tell Manfri you are here."

"Thank you."

Manfri came to me and embraced me, "Hello, darling! I am excited for you to see the show. Giovanni and his family will be joining you as VIP guests, so you needn't sit alone. Will our hairy son be crashing the show this evening?"

"Oh no, nai," I laughed. "Your mama said he can stay in here."

Manfri escorted her to her seat and said hello to Giovanni and his famailia. "Enjoy my friends and you as well, my beautiful wife." He kissed her and was off to fly!

The show was incredible with many oohs and aahs from the manush in the audience. After each family member had dismounted with a flourish, Manfri invited her once more to the center stage. "Ladies and gentlemen, some of you may have been here when I announced our engagement, now I would like you all to meet my lovely wife!" She took a bow.

Someone yelled, "Where is your hairy son?" There were roars of laughter.

He whistled and Beau came bounding out of the dressing area, jumping up and licking his master in the face, eliciting more laughter from the crowd. "As you can see, he has grown into a fine young man!" More laughter ensued. "Thank you all for joining us tonight and allowing us to entertain you doing something we love! Good evening from the entire Gambian family!"

The crowds began filing out and Giovanni told his family he would meet them at home later, he joined Manfri and I in the dressing area.

"Manfri, you are a splendid performer and so personable. The people love you!"

"Yes, they do. The show is amazing. I shall never tire of it. Perhaps I should join you on the flying trapeze?"

"Perhaps you should first give birth to our child! You would be quite a sight flying through the air with a large round belly!"

I told him, "I jest. I am actually afraid of heights."

"I learn something new about you every day, dear Crystobella. I would like to have some time alone with Giovanni tonight if you do not mind. I can walk you home and sneak out of the vardo at midnight."

"Perfect, yet, can you take me to Marcello's and then pick me up when you are on your way home? It will look like we were out together that way."

"Of course, perfect. Giovanni, our usual place at midnight?"

"See you then! Ta ta."

Chapter Thirty-Two

Later after being dropped at Marcello's door, I reveled in the comfort of his arms around me as we lay in bed. "Marcello, do you think one day we shall be able to be husband and wife in every sense of the word."

"Of course, mi amor. One day Claude will pass on as will Manfri's parents and we can live happily ever after."

"I am not sure that happily ever after exists outside of fairytales my love."

"It does if you believe it does, mi amor."

I laughed and rolled over on top of him and we made passionate love for the second time that night. In the wee hours of the morning there was a soft tap on the door and it was Manfri. Marcello called to her "Mi amor, your husband is here."

"Be there in a few moments, my love. Please ask him in."

Manfri would you like to come in and have a seat while you wait for Crystobella?"

"Thank you, Marcello, I would like that."

Marcello showed him to the kitchen and offered him a café. "I must decline your offer of kafa, but thank you for your hospitality. I must get some rest before our performance this afternoon."

"Of course, our nocturnal activities put a damper on our daily performance. Ah, Crystobella has arrived."

"I shall see you at the faire, my love."

"Yes, mi amor, I will see you later today." He kissed me goodbye and shook Manfri's hand. He stood in the doorway after showing us out and watched us walk away.

He wished his love could stay with him, and even knowing her husband was not into women, gave him no comfort when he saw them together. He witnessed Manfri putting his arm around her shoulders. They had a special bond that he did not approve of.

I was still feeling apprehensive about the dark force which was always present, just out of my reach. "Manfri, do you feel it?"

"Feel what?"

"The mamioro, what else?"

"No, I cannot say that I do. You still feel its presence?"

"Yes, I do, and it is gaining zor, it is mizhak."

He put his arm around me to comfort me. I lay my sero on his shoulder and we walked the rest of the way in silence.

"I must rest before the performance this afternoon, are you able to rest or must you go to the ofisa directly?"

"No, I shall rest for a few hours, the mornings are never busy and the ofisa is already set up." I crawled into my side of the bed and sov overtook me immediately.

He climbed in beside her; he thought I shall eventually get used to sleeping by her side. He too fell asleep within seconds of lying down.

They awoke a few hours later feeling refreshed. "I shall tend to the groi, would you like some breakfast afterward?"

"Yes, I would love that. What shall you cook?"

"Dudum and bokoli, it is Beau's favorite."

"Yes, of course you would make the rikono's favorite food," he laughed.

We shared a lovely breakfast and some chitchat.

"Crystobella, you are starting to show with child, I think we should get you a taliga to travel in."

"Manfri, do not worry, I shall be fine walking, it is good for me and the child."

"As you wish romni."

Chapter Thirty-Three

Later that day the group of women who had worked on my wedding day with me showed up for their free gifts. Jaunte' asked for a reading, the other three were more cautious and asked for bujos and crystals.

"I shall distribute the bujos and crystals before the reading so you may enjoy the reading while holding your personal protective pouches." I went to the table behind me and rummaged through the assorted crystals. I chose the first one. "For you Chantelle' I choose citrine, it is the stone of optimism. You have a cheerful personality, you are psychic, yet, you do not realize it, you are talkative and love to sing."

"Crystobella, you are correct! How do you do that, know me so well?"

"It is a gift," I handed the stone and bujo to Chantelle'.

Turning back to the selection I pulled out a moonstone. "For you Katie, a moonstone, it is the stone of clear thinking, it enhances psychic abilities and balances the emotions. I chose this because you have extremes in health, spirituality, and fortune. Service to others brings balance to your life as does moonstone to the emotions, you are also bold and beautiful like the moonstone."

"You are amazing! I dub you the amazing Crystobella!"

All of the women giggled and I continued. I produced another stone and handed it to Mary. "Your stone is the smoky-quartz. It is the stone of endurance, bringing serenity, calmness, and positive thought. You are at times rebellious, you have psychic power as well and you naturally bring joy to others, you are hard-working but a bit stubborn."

"I shall call you the amazing Crystobella as well! You are spot on, my dear."

"Now for you Jaunte', you may have a seat and put your hands next to mine on the crystal ball, please." Jaunte' did as she was asked.

I began to hum and I told Jaunte', "You are honest and benevolent, you are often intuitive. You have the gift, the gift of clairvoyance. You are bold, highly creative, and independent. You are philosophical, mature, determined, and intense with a desire to endure. You can be quite inquisitive and you love position and social status, these are important to you and you are always looking to improve your place in society. You know what you want in life and why you want it. I see you holding a key, this is the key to the material world, yet with this gift comes high spiritual responsibility. You must be true and fair to others. You are often religious or highly spiritual."

Jaunte' was staring at Crystobella with her mouth agape. "Yes, I am all of those things, but there must be more you have to tell me."

"Yes, let me pull some cards from the tarot for you." I shuffled the cards and asked Jaunte' to pass her hand over them three times. She did so. "The first card is the 9; the hermit. It is also the number of your soul. This card can represent God, fiery energy and life force. It stands for ageless wisdom and represents an open hand; you are the hand of God operating in the physical world. 9 is the completion of a cycle, it shows a lifetime of fulfillment with a dedication to service. You love more than most, yet, also may suffer more than most. You give more to people and often feel depletion afterward. You feel the need to establish universal love and a brotherhood of man. You must experience the power of letting go, non-attachment and go with the cosmic flow."

I turned over the next card. "It is the card 17 in the tarot and carries the energy of the 8 as well. 8 is your expression number. The star is the symbol for this card. You draw from the universe and gain revelation through meditation. You are above and beyond the elements; fire, air, earth, and water. You pour knowledge over humanity. 8 is a number of power and you reflect God's plan yet retain free-will and must choose between doing good or evil. You are protected and have a passion for justice being served."

I turned over the next card, "The 8 card, strength. 8 is also your personality number. You must elevate your kundalini energy to become more spiritual . . ."

Jaunte' asked, "What is kundalini?"

"It resides at the bottom of your spine like a coiled serpent; it is your life force."

"Oh my!" She exclaimed.

I continued. "You hold divine power and use it with gentleness and not with brute force."

I turned over the last card. "We have come to your final card. It is 5, the hierophant in the tarot. It is also your passion number. It symbolizes the inner teacher; intuition. You do not hear spirits for guidance but receive guidance from clairvoyance, the angels and the divine. You have wisdom and balance. You also can be restless and like to travel to relieve this sense of restlessness; you seek new experiences and love to meet new people. You engage your sixth sense; you are honest and expect the same from others. You do not like following rules and regulations, you are a free spirit and enjoy your freedom."

Jaunte said, "I love it, but how does this reading help me?"

"It gives you confirmation of your gifts and tells you how to use them. You know that you are gifted and yet you are not using these gifts to help others."

Jaunte' had a cloud of darkness come over her features and quickly recovered. "I must not be aware of these gifts, as you say. I am not sure what good this has done for me and I wish I would have chosen a crystal."

"You may deny these gifts or you may embrace them; the choice is certainly yours."

Just then Giovanni stepped inside of the ofisa. "I am sorry; I did not know you were busy. I shall return in a few moments. I will see if Marcello would like to join us as well. I shall return momentarily."

Jaunte' said, "Oh la la, I want him! You said I know what I want and why I want it, right? I think this reading was so I could meet him!"

"Well, yes, I did. I also said you like to elevate your social status and he would do so for you as he is the jeweler's son. Yet, I am afraid he is taken, married. Your honesty would not allow you to interfere with his relationship."

"Ah, well a girl can dream, can she not?"

"Of course, she can." I handed Jaunte' a stone, an emerald, as it is said to enhance psychic power. It also promotes self-knowledge. I gave a note to her with the stone, unnoticed from the others.

Jaunte' slipped outside while the other girls looked at Crystobella's wares, her lotions and potions and other stones.

Jaunte' began to read, *"I saw that you are also from the Gypsy heritage, you have turned your back on this heritage and have put your gifts away. You could do so much good with them and help others, it just takes courage. This is why you feel restless, you are a traveler, a nomad by birthright, and you are free to embrace your gifts or continue to turn your back on them. I just wish you to do what is best for the greatest good. Love Crystobella."* Jaunte' turned the emerald over and over in her hand, she knew Crystobella was correct as she did have the dook, the magic of the Gypsies, but unlike Crystobella she feared the consequences of letting people know that she did.

Marcello and Giovanni walked up at that moment; just as the others were leaving the ofisa. "Hello ladies," They both tipped their hats to them.

Despite Crystobella's warning, Jaunte' stuck out her hand as if she expected Giovanni to kiss it, "Hello, handsome. Did I not see you at the wedding of Manfri and Crystobella?"

He took her hand and shook it as he replied, "Yes, you did, and I remember you as well."

"Lovely, shall we go and get better acquainted at the café?"

"I am sorry, my dear, I have plans with these two lovely friends today."

"Perhaps another time then?"

"I am a married man, so I must decline your offer, miss."

I raised an eyebrow at her as if to say I told you so.

Just as they were about to walk away, Crystobella saw Mary looking at Marcello in a way she did not care for.

Mary stuck her hand out to Marcello, "We have met Giovanni, but who might you be?"

Marcello, being the gentleman that he is took her hand and kissed it lightly. "I am Marcello."

"My pleasure to meet you, sir."

I cut in, "I am sorry ladies but we have an appointment at this time, and my companions and I must take our leave. Good day."

As the trio walked off, we heard Mary exclaim, "Well, I never!"

Chapter Thirty-Four

I addressed my two male companions. It seems that the girls are sweet on you two, however do we explain who you are married to?" I contemplated this for a few moments. "I know! I shall tell them you are married to one another, it shall further our cause, and no one will think anything of us being seen as a threesome or foursome!"

"You are brilliant," said Giovanni.

"I am not sure I wish to have the town think I am married to a man!" Exclaimed Marcello.

"Now, now, my love. Who really cares what they think, we know the truth. I love you and that is all that matters." He nodded his agreement.

"Then it is settled, shall we go take our dinner?"

The two men flanked me and each hooked an arm as we went towards the café where Manfri was waiting for us. The men released me and I kissed my Dom's cheek. "Hello, husband!"

"Hello my pakvora romni!"

We all took our seats. Giovanni began to explain the situation of the infatuated women and how he and Marcello are now husband and husband. Manfri let out a loud laugh, "Splendid!"

Marcello retorted, "I am glad that you find it amusing!"

After we ate, everyone returned to our respective jobs. Marcello was in his booth at the faire and the woman named Mary approached him once more. "Hello," he said, "How may I help you?"

Claude was waiting at his daughter's ofisa. "I see you had many customers this morning, Baby Bear."

"It may have looked that way Papa, but I was repaying a monchimn't to the women who helped me at the wedding, as I had promised them."

"Crystobella, dear, we musn't give away our bread and butter."

"Yes, Papa, I understand. It will not happen again."

"Will you be coming home tonight?"

"I am not sure Papa, the vardo is unfinished, and Marcello has been so kind as to offer us his spare room until it is ready, so, we shall most likely be staying there once more."

"It is odd that you stay with him, the both of you, people will talk. You must be careful, Baby Bear; we want you to keep your head."

"Oh, Papa, they no longer use the guillotine, now I would be burned at the stake with a keg of gunpowder at my feet as not to suffer for long."

"Crystobella! Must you be so morbid?"

"I am sorry, Papa. Good day." I kissed him on his cheek and told him "I will be home the next day to cook for you after the faire."

"It will be nice to see you," he patted my shoulder and took his leave.

Marry looked around Marcello's tent, "I see you do woodworking. I have some things that need to be repaired in my home, are you available to do repairs?"

"I am sorry; I am previously occupied with jobs after the faire for quite some time."

"Well, if I did not know better, I would say you are trying your best to avoid my company."

"Mary, not that I am not flattered by your advances, yet, I am a married man."

"Yes, you say that, but you do not wear a ring. He pulled his coin from his shirt and said this is my token of commitment. I am a private man and do not like to advertise my business for all to see."

Mary persisted. "I see, well, I think you are just trying to fool me, why do you not wish to be with me?"

"Please, miss, if you have no further business, I must ask you to leave my tent."

"Well, I never! You will regret this!" She stomped off and he was glad to be rid of her.

That evening he relayed the story to Crystobella.

"I swear Marcello, she means trouble for us! I do not like her trying to seduce you!"

"Yes, she said as much."

"We must be on the watch for her, a woman scorned is dangerous."

Manfri came to get her early this night.

Marcello opened the door. "Hello, Manfri."

"Hello Marcello, how are you this night?"

"Well, except for the advances of Mary."

"Ah, yes, Giovanni is having the same problem with Jaunte', it is hard to explain a homosexual marriage, is it not?"

"Yes, it is, I do not envy you this."

"It seems we have switched places," Manfri laughed just as Crystobella came in.

"Hello Manfri," I kissed his cheek.

"Hello, darling."

"Can we stay here tonight, my dear?"

"Yes, if you wish, I would like to fetch Giovanni if we have a place to stay for the evening."

Marcello gave his assent. Manfri said, "We will be back soon."

"I shall have dinner ready for all of us, can you bring some wine?"

"Yes, but you shan't be drinking in your condition, are you?"

"Aye, Nai, it is for you men!"

He took his leave and I began to cook. Marcello stood behind me embracing me as I stirred the stew. We did not know that we were being watched.

Chapter Thirty-Five

Mary had been hiding in the wood waiting for her chance to spy on Marcello. She had seen the one named Manfri, come and go. *He is married to the witch*, she thought. *Whatever is he doing here at Marcello, the woodworker's house?* She crept through the shadows and spied in the window. What she saw made her gasp, she fell backward and was in fear of being heard or seen. She slipped back into the wood, where she was well hidden. She decided to wait for a bit and see what happened. She sat on the soft ground and leaned against a tree, she soon dozed off. Sometime later she was awakened by male voices. She peered through the trees and saw Manfri returning with Giovanni, they were holding hands! *Whatever is going on here*, she thought to herself.

Manfri knocked on the door and was let in by me, "Hurry come inside, I have the strangest feeling we are being watched."

"My darling, you always think we are being watched by the mamioro."

"Manfri, listen to me. This time it is not the mamioro, it feels like O zhuvindo. I felt the eyes of a female watching me while I cooked. Beau was whining and his hair is standing on end, he felt it as well."

"Are you sure it is not kesali? I think you are letting your imagination run away with you, my dear."

"Come and sit, both of you, the puyo is ready. There is pirogo for dessert. I know what I felt, Manfri, someone is watching us, they were sent by the mamioro, I am sure of that, he is using them to do his dirty work."

"This is far from appropriate supper talk. Shall we change the subject?"

"Yes, that would be nice," Said Giovanni.

So, she is a witch, she can feel me watching her. I knew it today when we were at the fortune-telling-tent with her. Mary continued to watch the four of them from the shadows near the window. Marcello began to have a fit and the witch ran to get a vial, she poured something down his throat and he stopped, he seemed to return to normal. She has possessed him, no wonder he will not give Mary any attention, he is under her spell!

She wanted to gather as much evidence as possible before she went to the constable, so she continued to watch them late into the night. What she saw made her skin crawl, they were a lot of heathens, all of them, a coven, and they were having an orgy! Well she saw them all hug and kiss after dinner and then they retired, she could not see, but she could hear them. She ran from the wood to her home, tomorrow she would alert the constable and the parish priest.

Our foursome said our goodnights and retired to our prospective bedrooms; we were all experiencing ecstasy if anyone were there to hear us. I, longed to see Manfri with his lover, yet, I knew Marcello would not approve, so I covered the sounds coming from my husband's room with my own.

That night Mary had a nightmare. She saw the four of them from the coven engaged in sexual acts of perversion and she awoke feeling disgust! She could not wait until they all were burned at the stake; it was less than they deserved. She dressed hurriedly and went into the towne; her first stop was the parish house. She knocked hard and the housekeeper let her in. Mary called out before the housekeeper could take her leave, "Father Bovary! Please I must see you now!"

He came from his office looking flustered. "What is it Mary?"

"I need you to come with me to report a coven of witches to the constable."

"What? Who?"

"The newlyweds, Manfri and Crystobella, along with their consorts Marcello and Giovanni!"

"My dear, you must be mistaken, they have just been here to file their registry and I found all of them quite pleasant. They cannot be witches."

"I tell you; I saw it with my own two eyes. I was hiding in the wood near the house of Marcello. He was inside when Manfri arrived. I saw Manfri go into the house and then leave. He left without his wife and I knew she was there; I had seen her in the yard earlier. I decided to see what was going on inside, I saw the wife of Manfri, Crystobella cooking at the stove . . ."

"My dear child, cooking is not a crime of witchcraft."

"Father, please, let me continue."

He nodded, "Of course, go on."

"Marcello was behind her with his arms around her kissing her neck."

"Well adultery is a crime, but not one associated with witchcraft."

"I know, father, but I hid in the wood and fell asleep near a tree, I was awakened later by voices, I saw Manfri returning with Giovanni, they were holding hands. The witch let them in and . . ."

"By witch, do you mean Crystobella?"

"Yes. She let them in and they sat down to dinner. They were eating chicken stew, I saw her perform the ritual of killing the chicken in the yard earlier while I was in the wood, and Marcello began to have fits, she, the witch got up and grabbed a small vial and poured something in his mouth, soon after he was normal again. She has possessed him, I tell you, she has cast a spell on them all!"

"Calm yourself girl. Was there any more witchcraft that you witnessed?"

"I heard the rest. They all finished dinner, they even allowed the dog to eat from a bowl! Then they embraced one another and kissed one another, they were preparing for an orgy!"

"Oh, my lord, how do you know this?"

"I heard them having relations and making all sorts of sounds, then later that night the devil put a dream into my head and I saw the orgy! It was frightful, Father, they must be punished!"

"Let us go to the constable, he will know what to do."

Chapter Thirty-Six

They arrived at the constable's office. Father Bovary said, "Constable, we are here to make accusations against a coven of witches. This is highly unusual, but there are four of them and three of them are men. We believe that the female witch has cast a spell over them or taken possession of them. She gave a vial to one of the men and he came out of a fit, that proves possession and that she can control when it takes him over. Then they all had sexual relations with one another."

The constable thought about it and said, "We need more evidence before we can take them into custody."

Mary piped up, "Well, yesterday I went to the fortune-telling-tent of the witch, and she gave me a charm, something she calls a bujo. She had many potions in her tent as well, and herbs. She did a reading for me and my friends. She told us we were all clairvoyant and were not using our gifts. Then Marcelo denied my attention and Giovanni denied Jaunte's affection. The witch has them under her spell and they are now like her."

"Do you have the charm?"

Mary pulled it from her pocket, "Yes, it is here," she thrust her hand at him, and when she opened her palm, he saw a small pouch with herbs inside and a gemstone. "Did she say this had magic inside of it?"

"Not exactly, but she said it would protect us."

"I will need this as evidence," he took it from her palm. "Can your friends corroborate your story? If they file a complaint, we will have the two or more necessary to ask for the death penalty."

Mary said, "I am sure that Chantelle' and Katie would. I do not know if Jaunte' will as she is very big on honesty and did not see anything with her own eyes."

The constable asked her, "Would you please go and bring your friends to me at once."

She told him, "I will be back with them as soon as possible." She fled from the building and was gone in a flash.

I arose in the morning and stretched, let Beau out to relieve himself and saw something shining on the ground near the kitchen window. I walked over and picked it up. It was a charm from a bracelet, as I turned it over in my hand, I knew I had seen it before. In a flash I saw the owner and how she had obtained the charm on her eighteenth birthday, and it belonged to Mary. It still held her energy. I thought; *how did it get there?* I would have to return it to Mary and have a talk with her. I stuck it in my posoti and whistled for Beau. I returned to the house and made some breakfast for the men. A nice scrambled egg dish with garlic and herbs, some toast and kafa. "Boys, your breakfast is ready!"

They came in one by one and sat down. I kissed Marcello, and told the men I had promised Papa to deliver breakfast and I needed to tend the horses before I left for the faire. 'I shall go now to see him before I arrive at the faire."

Manfri said, "It is best if I accompany you to the kumpania, will you wait just a moment?"

"Yes, I shall have a bit of ginger tea. My stomach is a bit off this morning, it seems our child does not like it when I eat early in the day."

After breakfast, Manfri took her arm in his and they set out for her father's camp. Marcello had told her he and Giovanni would go to the faire and they could all meet for dinner as they had yesterday.

"Manfri, do you think our child will be a boy or a girl?"

"I had not given it much thought; either is fine with me, I guess. I know my mother would love a grand-daughter as she has only had me, a son up until now."

"I would like one as well, but I am sure Papa would love a boy, he has never had a son. I guess we shall just wait and see when the child blesses us with its birth."

"When we arrived at the camp, the horses were restless; I went to them and calmed them. I gave them some hay and grain and went to fetch pani nevi.

Manfri called to me. "Yes, dom?"

"You go wake your father so his breakfast does not get cold and I will give the horses their pani."

"Thank you, darling," I said as I went to my father's vurdon. Beau bounded up the steps and went inside in front of me. He licked Claude's face and I laughed. "Papa, Beau seems to be affectionate toward you."

He mumbled something as he wiped his cheeb. "Very funny, Baby Bear." He swatted at Beau to go away.

"Papa, I have brought you your breakfast. Please join us by the fire; I will make you some kafa."

"Yes, Crystobella, I will be out."

"Do not be long I must leave for the faire soon." I went to the fire and saw a jar of pertia.

"Oh, my, poor Papa he has taken to eating these disgusting pig parts!" I prepared the djezbeh and set it on the fire.

Manfri and Beau joined me and soon after Papa came and took a seat. "Papa, is this your supper from last night?" I held up the pertia.

"Yes, some of us consider this a delicacy."

"Next time you do not have a good supper, please come join us at Marcello's."

"Why are the two of you staying there? You should be here in your vardo."

"Yes, sir, we know, but it is not ready to live in and Marcello has been gracious enough to offer his spare room. It is comfortable and we will move in here as soon as we finish the vardo." Manfri explained.

"I see," said Claude, "Very well then."

We bid farewell to Claude. "Bye, Papa, I will see you tonight for supper when I come to feed the horses. I shall wait here for Manfri to come before going to Marcello's, we would not want the towne to talk about us, it is better if we go there together."

Manfri shook his hand and patted him on the back the way men do. "See you tonight Claude."

We walked hand in hand to keep up appearances. There was a light easy banter between us as we went.

Chapter Thirty-Seven

Mary returned to the constable's office with two of her friends in tow, "Jaunte' refused to be a part of this 'nonsense' as she called it," she explained to the constable. "This is Chantelle' and Katie. The witch gave each of them a charm as well and could read their minds."

"Is this true, ladies?" They both nodded.

"Katie spoke up, "I think she is trying to put a spell on Jaunte' and make her be a part of her coven; she passed her a note with a beautiful gemstone. Jaunte' looked shaken after reading it."

The constable said, "I will need to take that note from her and put it into evidence can one of you show me where she lives?"

Mary volunteered.

She led the way to Jaunte's house with the Priest, the Constable, and her two friends behind her.

The constable knocked on the door. When she answered he addressed her, "Miss, we must take the letter you have in your possession, given to you by the accused witch and the gemstone as well."

"I am sorry, Constable, I have thrown them into the river, I wanted nothing to do with her note or her charms," she lied.

Mary pointed a finger at her. "You have a spell cast upon you by her! I never saw you throw anything into the river."

"Mary, please do not be absurd, you are letting hysteria take control of you."

"You have become one of them, so you can have Giovanni in your bed, you are willing to sacrifice your soul and give it to the devil to be with him!"

She said to her friend before slamming the door, "You are the one who is possessed; I have done no such thing!"

The constable knocked on her door, "Miss, I am afraid you are going to have to come with me, "We are holding you on suspicion of witchcraft." He grabbed her arm as she tried to shut the door once more and she struggled to free herself. He dragged her from her home and pushed her down the street toward the police station as she screamed.

"Mary! Have you gone mad? They will kill me!"

Mary just smiled. When they got to the police station, she saw that her charm was missing from her bracelet. She told the constable, "I believe the witch took my charm to put a curse on me, you will find it in her possession when you go to collect her."

Jaunte' continued to scream as she was put in the stockade for all of the towne to witness her persecution.

Manfri and I heard the commotion and went to investigate.

Mary yelled, "There is the witch, get her, and her consort!"

The pair turned to run but the constable and one of his deputies grabbed them. They were thrust into the stockades as well.

I sobbed, "We are expecting our first child, why are you doing this? Please release us, these accusations are not true! Please!" I begged.

Manfri was in shock. He looked as if he was going to faint. I know I looked hopeless, and the constable reached into my posoti and took out the charm, tearing my skirt in the process, saying, "You were correct, she does have your charm, Mary."

I could see clearly what was on Mary's soul. She wanted Marcello so badly that when she could not have him, she went to his house to spy on him and see why. I knew then that the mamioro had possessed her mind and put her up to this; he even had her turn on her friend. In the end he shall win and reclaim his child. I began to sob.

Soon a crowd was forming in front of the Police station. The crowd were throwing things and taunting us. It was a nightmare that only grew worse when Manfri's parents came to see what was happening.

"Oh my God, No!" Screamed Claire.

"What is the meaning of this?" Bellowed Antonio. He stormed into the constable's office.

The constable explained the situation to him and Antonio said, "You will not win, I shall find a barrister and we shall sue the towne!" He stomped out of the station and grabbed his wife's hand, tearing her away from the horrid site of their son and his family being persecuted in the towne square.

Claude came by with Marcello and Giovanni to see what the ruckus was in the towne as no one was attending the faire; they were all standing around the square.

Mary saw them and yelled, "There are the other two consorts! Get them!"

The deputies went and grabbed them before they knew what was happening. Marcello and Giovanni were added to the collection hanging in the stockades.

Marcello looked at his love, "Mi amor, I love you," was all he said before hanging his head.

I knew this was the end for all of us and poor Jaunte', her only crime is her infallible sense of justice. We were all to die and there was nothing anyone could do to help us. The only crime committed here was that a woman was rejected by a married man. Yes, a woman scorned is the devil herself, but such an accusation would only cement the death of me and my child.

Giovanni looked out of place in his nice suit hanging in the stockade. His suit was now stained with tomatoes and horse manure that had been thrown at us. He looked to Manfri and began to cry.

Manfri no longer cared what anyone thought of his homosexuality, "My love, I will see you on the other side, never doubt my love for you."

I searched the crowd for my father. He was nowhere to be found. Yes, the coward must have run. He probably has hitched-up my beloved horses and is fleeing towne right this very moment. I felt the greatest sadness come over me, not because I was going to die, but because I was not loved by my own father. In the end his selfishness won.

Beau ran to the tserha of the familia Gambian, Claire found him huddled by the shoshka. He was shaking, "Poor baby," she murmured. "I must let Crystobella know he is safe no matter how my heart breaks seeing my family like that." She walked back to the towne centre.

"Crystobella, Beau is safe in our tent, I shall care for him. I love you all!" She turned and ran as her zor faded. Tears streamed from her eyes.

Chapter Thirty-Eight

That evening the five witches were brought into the jail. Papers had been filed with the magistrate for a pre-trial. Antonio and Giovanni's father had secured the best barrister's in France. Although with the mass hysteria that ran rampant in a witch trial, they feared the worst. Not all witch trials ended with a death sentence, but the witches were tortured and if they confessed there would be little the barristers could do.

Jaunte' was chained to the wall and she was only lashed, they were not going to give her the death penalty, they just wanted her confession against the others. She refused of course.

I heard her screams as they lashed her over and over. They threw her back in the cell and grabbed Giovanni, I went to her to comfort her, "Please tell them that I gave you the charm and where it is, and please do not let them torture you anymore."

"I shan't! You are not a witch; Mary is a poor loser. I am so sorry that I brought her with us, please forgive me Crystobella."

"Shush, I forgive you. I shall pray for you."

"And I for you." Jaunte' passed out from her pain and I sat cradling her head for what seemed like hours as I listened to Giovanni scream.

They threw him back in all bloody and I began to weep for my friends. I felt helpless, I cursed the mamioro. "If you were not dead mamioro, I would kill you myself!"

They grabbed Manfri and I tried to hold him by his arm, but they ripped it from me.

Marcello put his arms around me, "Be strong, mi amor, be strong, and know that I love you."

"Know that I love you, Marcello, and know that if I thought it would save you, I would give you to Mary," she sobbed.

"Nonsense, mi amor, I would rather face death than to be with her and without you."

"I love you with all of my heart and soul and we shall meet again in another life. I promise you that."

He kissed my head before they drug him out as well. I broke down and began to hyperventilate, *why both of them*? I heard them being tortured, I could not imagine what they were doing to them. When they were thrown back into the cell, I saw that they had been scalded with boiling water and their fingers had been broken.

They grabbed me. "We saved the best for last, witch, it is your turn."

They put my head in a witches bridle, a torture device that looked like a cage and had four sharp prongs that inserted into the mouth, two on the tongue and one on each cheeb, they locked it to my head and I felt the warm blood fill my mouth as the prongs pierced through my flesh and tongue. They put my arms above my head and hung me from the wall. I went within and blocked out the pain. I began to pass out from the pain and they lashed me with a leather strap that had small metal studs embedded in it, they would not allow me to sleep. When morning arrived, they undid my torture device and let me down. I felt the blood rush to my arms, and it hurt. I began to lie on the floor and cry, "I will say whatever you want, please do not harm my friends anymore, promise me, and I will tell you what you wish to know."

"Are you a witch?"

"No, I am a healer, a Gypsy . . ."

"Liar, you are a witch, tell us what we want to know or we will bring your men back and mutilate their genitals."

"I am a witch, I am a witch, I practice magick, but my friends are not, please let them go."

"Have you possessed them?"

"No!"

"Guards, bring the men and get the scalpels ready . . ."

"No, I will tell you the truth! I did, I possessed them, I wanted them for myself . . ." I began to pass out and the guard kicked me, I cried out in pain.

"Did you and they sacrifice animals in your yard during your Sabbaths and perform orgies?"

"What . . . I . . . do not know what you are . . ." I was kicked once more. "Yes, yes, we did," I gasped.

"Good that is what we needed to know so we can put you to death, all except the other woman, we know you were recruiting her and she will be imprisoned for one year."

"No, you said if I told you what you wanted, they would be spared! No! Nai! Please!"

They threw me in the cell and looked at Juante', "We shall have fun with you over the next year, yes, we shall."

Jaunte' began to cry and told the others they had already raped her savagely and stuck things in her that hurt her. She would rather die with the rest of us than endure that torture again. She called to the guards "I want to confess!"

"Confess to what?"

"I am also a witch, I was one before Crystobella approached me, I performed the rituals with them in Marcello's yard, I am as guilty as they are."

"Then you shall join them in hell."

The announcement of the burnings spread through the towne like wild fire! It was set for the following day.

Antonio and Lorenzo came to the station, "You cannot do this!"

"We can and we will. The witches have confessed, we no longer need the magistrate to hold a trial."

"This is not possible; they did not practice witchcraft!"

"They confessed. They will be burned tomorrow. See you there." They sneered at the men. "If you do not leave, you may join them." The pair left with their heads hanging. They knew they were defeated. Antonio hung a sign on his tent '*All shows cancelled until further notice.*'

Chapter Thirty-Nine

Lorenzo told his wife, Sofia, he has decided that they would be going back to Italy. He could no longer be in the town that murdered his son. She broke down and begged him to stay until after the burnings.

"You cannot possibly want to see your son burned to death." He looked at her aghast.

"He must know we were there until the end; he must see our face full of love as he leaves this earth."

"Yes, my love, we shall stay for him and then we are to leave immediately for the old world."

Antonio told Claire that they must let Manfri know they are there for him, in the end, no matter how hard it will be and then they will tear down the tent and move on to another city, they cannot bear to stay here any longer, the memories will be too hard on their hearts.

Claire asked him, "Have you seen Claude?"

"I saw him in the crowd at the stockades and I did not see him after that."

Maybe we should go and support him, let him know we are here for him, after all, we are now familia. They set out for Claude's camp. When they arrived, they saw only the new vardo that belonged to Manfri and Crystobella, the camp was empty of the horses and Claude and his vurdon. He had fled.

"What a coward that man is," said Antonio, "Abandoning his daughter when she needs him most!"

Claire said, "Crystobella will know we are here for her. My beautiful daughter, I just found her and now she and my beloved Manfri are being taken from us! She went to the vardo and her husband followed her, they went inside and she wept, and they prayed. When she was spent, she whispered to her husband, "May we go now?"

"He took her by the hand and answered her, "Yes, my love, we may go, we must have much zor for tomorrow."

The group being held in the jail could hear the work being done in preparation for their executions, the horse wagons were hauling wood up to the hill, and men were yelling directions as to where things were to be built. It was terrifying to think that tomorrow they would all be burned to death, and for what? A woman scorned, a woman who allowed hysteria to take over when her emotions were already running high. We sat in a circle and began to pray, "Our father who art in heaven, hallowed be thy name, thy kingdom come on earth as it is in heaven, give us this day our daily bread and forgive our trespasses, as we forgive those who trespass against us, and lead us not into temptation, but deliver us from evil, for thine is the power, the kingdom, and the glory forever and ever amen."

A guard came in and laughed at them, "You think you can repent now, do you, it won't work, you will soon meet the dark lord you worship, you will see Satan up close, and personal, you will!"

I began to weep, for my child as well as for my friends and for myself. I prayed that my child would not feel the pain of the flames. I begged God, *"Please, God, protect this child from the pain of burning, take this child and place it in the arms of angels so that it may not suffer . . ."* I could no longer speak and Marcello put his arms around me and we wept together.

Giovanni spoke to Jaunte', "You were saved, you would have only to spend a year in prison, and then you would be freed, but you chose to die with us. Why did you do this?"

"I would rather die than be at the mercy of those ignorant men for the next year. I could not stand to have them touch me one more time or do those unspeakable things to me again."

I asked her, "What things?"

"Were they not done to you? They stuck things inside of me until I bled, they raped me one after another . . ." she began to sob so hard that she could no longer speak."

I answered her, "No, they did not, I only wish that they had so that the child I carry may have been spared the torture of burning to death within my womb."

"Oh, no, I am so sorry, Crystobella, I did not know that you were expecting." She said through her tears.

Giovanni comforted her by holding her in his arms. They knew the time was drawing near and Manfri sat with his arm around his love, soon I and Marcello joined them and we sat together in a circle while embracing one another. Each took a turn telling the one thing they want known before they die.

Jaunte' said, "I want all the people to know I am a Gypsy. I have hidden my heritage all of my life and I will now proudly claim who and what I am."

I went next. "I have always been who and what I was born to be, and I will tell each and every one of you that I love you with all of my heart and soul, and that love will last through eternity. We shall meet again, in another lifetime and our hearts will remember our connection."

Giovanni spoke next. "I wish all to know that I am a homosexual and giving my love to a man does not make me any less human. I love you all."

Manfri went next. "I love you all as well, and Crystobella, even though you are a woman, I felt a bond with you, I am in love with Giovanni, yet, I felt something equally strong with you."

I kissed him on the cheek. "Thank you my, friend, I felt the same bond."

Marcello spoke last. "I would like to thank Manfri and Giovanni for what they sacrificed to allow me to be with mi amor de mi vida. I love you Crystobella with a love that transcends time and space. I extend that love to all of you who will share in this great trauma we shall suffer, but in the end we will all gain the freedom we have been searching for. Goodbye my friends." Just then we heard the guard coming.

Chapter Forty

"I have your families here to say their last goodbyes and give you the gunpowder if you wish to put it around your neck to speed things up a bit."

Claire and Antonio were there along with Lorenzo, Sophia, and Jaunte's aunt, Ines, with whom she resided. They were each allowed a turn to hug their loved one through the bars and hand them the gun powder bag, the whole process was very sad and filled with tears.

When it came time for Claire, she told me, "I shall always love you as my own daughter and I do not blame you for any of this." She handed me the bag of gunpowder, as she knew Claude had left and was not here to give her one to help ease the suffering.

I thanked her and kissed her cheek, "I love you, Dya."

The guard rushed them out of the holding area and told them, "The prisoners will be paraded through the towne in two hours' time, before being taken to the burning hill. Better come early to get good seats." He sneered.

Claire spat in his face as she passed him. The families went directly to the church to beg the priest to pardon their children, but he had barricaded himself inside of his office and would not answer their cries, they went to the pulpit and kneeled, each lighting a candle in honor of their loved one and then they prayed for the next two hours.

The guard took the prisoners out in a line shackled to one another, they had been given light white cotton clothing to wear, which resembled nightgowns. They were given chains to hang their gunpowder around their necks. He led them to the main street and paraded them around the square with three other guards to ensure they did not escape. There were crowds of people, and small children played games, the people were excited for tonight's festivities it seemed. There were cherry vendors and men selling pickles, there were even tents selling beer.

I felt disgusted and sick to my stomach, I vomited in the street and for that received a kick from the nearest guard.

When we were led up the burning hill the crowds were cheering even louder. I saw the massive wooden stakes with the thick layers of logs beneath each one, and in between each layer of thick logs was a layer of straw and brush. Straw, brush, and thin twigs were then set in a teepee fashion over the entire pyre, with enough room to ensure that oxygen could get in to fuel the flames; I heard Jaunte' gasp behind me.

One by one we were chained to the wooden stakes with our shackles and a rope tied around our mid-section to make sure we did not have room to move. The towne's people then were allowed to throw eggs and tomatoes at us. I saw the towne diplomats and those that were considered important seated to my right in a special area with comfortable chairs and tables, wenches were serving drinks and food to the aristocrats. I searched the crowd for Claire, Antonio, Lorenzo, Sophia, and Ines; I saw them huddled by a tree far to the left of the crowds. I felt empathy for what they were going to have to endure tonight. I was somewhat relieved that Claude had abandoned me; at least he will be spared this atrocious spectacle. I silently forgave him his trespasses.

After some time, the executioner was ready to light the pyres. He started at the left side where Giovanni was on the end, next in line was Manfri, then Marcello, I came next, and last was Juante'. I smelled the sickening smell of flesh beginning to burn just as the torch was touched to my pyre. I could hear the screams beginning on my left, then the sickening explosion of the bags of gun powder, one by one and the terrifying screams that accompanied them. my gunpowder bag exploded pelting my face with white hot pellets of metal, and I screamed aloud with the pain. I began to pray and just as Jesus had done before me, I cried out to the crowd. "I forgive you all, for you know not what you do!" I felt the flames lapping at my skin, my flesh was beginning to sear, next it became charred as my muscles began to cook and my blood to boil, the oil from my melting fat fueled the fire and it became hotter. It was now just a matter of seconds before I would be gone, and then it was so.

I floated above my body. I saw the charred remains and the wooden stake began to crumble and fall. I began to float upward on a shaft of light. I saw my mother and grandmother waiting at the top with outstretched arms to welcome me home and I knew that I would indeed be reunited with my loved ones who perished with me this fateful day.

Claire, Sophia, and Inez clung to one another trying to console the inconsolable. Antonio hung his head into his hands and sobbed for the entire world to see. Lorenzo screamed to the crowd, "WHAT HAVE YOU DONE?" Before passing out and falling to the ground. Their lives would never be the same. Claire thought about Claude, where was he, how could he have abandoned his daughter in her greatest time of need? The crowds began to thin and the families made their way to their respective homes.

Claude was hidden in the wood just behind the place where the pyres had stood. He was weeping inconsolably and he vowed he would always be by his daughter's side to protect her in every lifetime to come.

Epilogue

Fade to the present: I experienced this lifetime very deeply, most likely because Claude was near, keeping the energy and memories alive within me. I am grateful for everything I experienced in that life and even more grateful that Claude was finally freed from his self-induced sentence of guarding me for eternity.

I have met one of the people I was with in that lifetime; his name ironically in this lifetime is Marcello. I was drawn to him like a moth to a flame and we spent five very passionate years together before parting ways. Whatever we had had before was not the same in this lifetime, and I suspect we had had other lifetimes before this one that created the shift in our karmic relationship. I am certain it was he though. I believe that I have met the others as well, maybe I just did not recognize them for who they were, but I always recognize those that are soul-mates, and I have an affinity for gay men in this lifetime, and now I know why, Manfri and Giovanni!

Until next time when we meet again! Stay Blessed!

Travellers, towne, and faire are misspelled on purpose as this is how Gypsies or the Roma

spell them.

A votre santé/ (to your health, live long, a

toast) (French)

Abiav/ (a wedding Feast)

Adieux/ (good day) (French)

Adre /(inside)

Ambrols/ (Pears)

Amirya/ (curse)

Ando foro/ (into towne)

Angustris/ (rings)

Arter/ (after)

Bal/ (hair)

Barearav/ (honor and respect)

 Baro/ (large)

Barri/ (big)

 Barvalimos/ (wealth)

Bater/ (may it be so)

Baxtalo/ (happy)

Beng /(devi

Berk/ (breasts)

Besh/ (sit)

Bibaxt/(bad luck)

Binak/ (twin)

Binos/ (transgressions)

Bobas/ (beans)Bogacha/ (baked flour bread)

Bokoli/ (thick pancakes stuffed with

small pieces of meat)

Bolta/ (shop)

Bon appétit/ (Good Appetite,

salutation before eating) (French)

Bon après-midi/ (Good After noon)

(French)

Bonjour/ (Hello) (French)

Bori/ (bride or daughter-in-law)

Bov/(oven)

Braski/ (frogs)

Buino/ (proud)

Bujo/(medicine bag, pouch)

but guli/ (sweets)

Butji /(possession)

Chachimos /(truth)

Chakano /(star)

Chao/ (tea)

Chavi/(child)

Cheeb/ (tongue)

Chere/ (stars)

Chey/(daughter or girl)

Chiez/ (dowry)

Chin/(cut)

Chor/ (thief)

Choribe/ (stealing)

Chote /(vinegar)

Chovexani/ (witch)

Chuchis/ (breasts)Darane svatura/ (superstitions or

magical)

Daro/ (bride price)

Dat/ (father)

Devel/ (God)

Dickler/ (neck scarf)

Dicklo/ (head scarf of a married

woman)

Didikai/ (Gypsy friend)

Dila /(floor)

Djezbeh/ (coffee pot)

Dom /(husband)

Doodah/ (sweetmeat)

Dook/ (magic or sight)

Drab/ (herbs)

Draba /(charms)

Drabarno/ (fortune teller)

Drarnego/ (herbal medicine or

special healing herb)

Drom/ (way)

Dudum/ (melon)

Dya /(mother, mama)

Familia/ (family or extended family)

Familiyi/ (extended family formal)

Ferari/ (blacksmith)

Fusui eski zumi/ (butter bean soup)

Ga/ (walk)

Gabori/ (jeweler)

Gajengi baxt/ (bad-luck, luck of a

non-gypsy)

Gajo/ (non-gypsy man)

Galbi/(gold medallion)Gelo/ (gone)

Glasso/ (varieties of Gypsy music)

Gooi/ (pudding)

Grai/(Horse)

Groi or Groy/ (horses)

Jekhipe/ (unity, and oneness)

jil avree/ (go away)

Kafa/ (coffee)

Kanny/ (chicken)

Kar/ (penis)

Karbaro/ (big penis)

Kasht/ (forest or woods)

Kasko san/ (whose are you)

Katrinsa/ (apron)

Kazan/ (small, copper still)

Keres/ (what is going on here)

Kertsheema/ (tavern)

Kesali/ (forest spirit)

Kham/(sun)

Khania /(hens)

Khushti/ (good)

Kintala/ (balance)

Kirvi/ (groom)

Kishti/ (belt)

Kocho/ (button)

Kohl/ (charcoal)

Kokalo/ (bone)

Komi/ (more)

Kon/ (who)

Koshter/(stick)kris Romani/ (trial of Gypsy elders)

Kumpania/ (group of Gypsies living

together)

Lashav/ (shame, embarrassment,

disgrace

Lavuta/ (violin)

Led/ (ice)

Lel/ (arrest)

Lolo mura/ (strawberries)

Lon/ (salt)

Love/ (money)

Lovina/ (beer)

lungo drom/ (long road)

Machka/ (cat)

Mahala/ (quarter)

Mal/(bad)

Mamioro/ (a spirit bringing serious

illness)

Mang/ (beg)

Manus/ (man)

Manush/ (people)

Mariki/ (mariki (a sweet, layered,

pizza-shaped pastry from flour, powdered

milk, sugar, and bread)

Marime/ (defiled)

Mashakar/ (waist or centre)

Ma-sha-llah/ (as God wills)

Maw! /(exclamation!)

Mi amor! /(my Love) (Spanish)

Mira/Miri/(My)

Miro/ (quiet)

Mish/ (vagina)Mizhak /(wicked)

Mon chèri/(My darling) (French)

Monashay/ (wife)

Monchimo/ (debt)

Moro/ (bread)

Mort/(woman)

mortsi /(leather)

Muj/ (face)

Mulani/ (ghost)

Mule/ (spirit)

mule-vi/ (medium)

Mulla/ (corpse)

Muller'd gajo/ (murdered non-gypsy

man)

Muller'd/ (killed or murdered)

Mulo/(spirit of the dead)

Mush/ (man)

Nak/ (nose)

Nano/ (uncle)

Narky/ (bad, unpleasant)

Naswalemos/ (illness)

Natsia/ (Gypsy nation, race, or tribe)

Natsiyi/ (Tribe of Roma)

Nav-romano/ (Gypsy name)

Nevipe/(news)

Niamo/ (relatives)

Nivasi/ (water spirits)

O zhuvin (the live one)

Ofisa/ (fortune telling tent)

Opre/ (arise)Pahome/ (frozen)

Pakiv, dav pakiv (respect, obey,

honor and esteem)

Pakvora/ (beautiful)

Pani nevi/ (fresh Water)

Paramishus/ (tale)

Paramitsha/ (gypsy fairytale)

Parno/ (white)

Patisserie/(Pastry Shop) (French)

Perina/ (blanket, quilt)

Pertia/ (jellied pig's feet and ears)

Petalos/(shoes)

Phuro/ (elder)

Pi/ (drank)

Pibe (s)/(drink(s))

Pirogo/ (Noodle and cheese

pudding)

Pliashka/ (engagement party and

bottle of good brandy wrapped in a kerchief

with a string of gold pieces)

Popin-mas / (goose-meat)

Porado/ (erection)

Posoti /(pocket)

Potchee/ (pocket)

Prikasa or Prikaza/ (bad luck or very

bad omen)

Puri Daj/

(grandmother,grandmamma)

Putain gitane/(Gypsy Whore)

(French)

Puyo/ (chicken stew)

Rahat lokum/ (Food)Rakli/ (girl)

Rat/ (blood)

Rawnie/ (lady)

Ray Baro/ (Great Lord)

Rebniko/ (pond)

Rinkeni/ (attractive)

Rikono/ (dog)

Roj/ (spoon)

Rom Baro/ (Gypsy leader

Romanes/ (Romani language)

Romania/ (Gypsy laws)

Romania/ (social order, laws, and

traditions of the gypsy)

Romni (Wife)

Romnipen/ (Gypsyhood)

Rovliako khelipen/ (stick dance)

Ruv/ (wolf)

Ryes/ (gentlemen)

Sar san Kako/ (How are you Uncle)

Sar san/ (how are you)

Sarma/ (stuffed cabbage)

Sastimos or Sastimos schej /(a

greeting, to your health, Gypsy girl)

Sastimos/(enjoy)

Sastro/ (father-in-law)

Satarmas/ (stars)

Saviako/(rolled pastry with fruit and

cottage cheese)

Schav/ (Gypsy boy)

Seros/ (heads)

Shanglo/ (constable or police)Shav/ (push)

Shavora/ (companions)

Shera/ (head)

Sheranda/ (goosedown stuffed

pillows covered in floral material)

Shilmulo/ (vampire)

Shon/ (moon)

Shoshka/ (tent pole)

Sir/ (garlic)

Skorni/ (top boot)

Slobuzenja/ (freedom)

sov /(sleep)

stanya/ (stable)

streyino/ (strange)

sumadji/ (family heirloom)

Tablipen/ (warmth)

Tachiben/ (truth)

Tacho/ (true)

Talig/a (two wheeled light cart)

Tan/ (market).

Tarneder/ (younger

Tato/ (warm or heat)

Tenimos/ (youth)

Thoximos/ (duty)

Tisane/ (herbal tea)

Tserha/ (tent)

Tumnimos/ (Betrothal)

Vardo /(wagon for living in)

Vast/ (hand)

Veshengo/ (man of the forest) vezlime'/ (embroidered)

Vista/ (kin or clan)

Vurdon/ (wagon)

Waver/ (woods)

Wortacha/partners

Xa/ (eat)

Xaimoko/ (rabbit stew)

Xanimiki/ (co-parents in law)

Xari/ (one who eats)

Xarits/a (fried cornbread)

Yog /(fire)

Zen/ (saddle)

Zhamutro/ (Son-in-law)

Zheita/ (bringing the bride home)

Zor/ (strong or strength)

Made in the USA
Monee, IL
21 October 2021